Just thinking about three
long nights playing poker
with the prettiest lawyer
west of the Mississippi made
Clayton Black's skin tingle.

There were some things about Irene Hardisson he'd give
his eyeteeth to know—like what she thought about at
night. What she wanted in life. What she looked like
underneath all those flounces.

That settled it. He'd stay. For a while. A *short* while.
Might do him good to hang his hat somewhere he was
actually wanted for a change. But she was no rambling
rose. She was a lady and he wouldn't compromise her.
And he'd work damn hard to keep her from sticking in
his memory when he rode away.

Praise for Lynna Banning's previous titles

PLUM CREEK BRIDE

"...pathos and humor blend in a plot that glows
with perception and dignity."
—*Affaire de Coeur*

WILDWOOD

"5 ★s."
—*Heartland Critiques*

WESTERN ROSE

"...warm, wonderful and witty—
a winning combination from a bright new talent."
—*Award-winning author Theresa Michaels*

The Law and Miss Hardisson
Harlequin Historical #537—November 2000

The Law and Miss Hardisson

LYNNA BANNING

HARLEQUIN®

TORONTO • NEW YORK • LONDON
AMSTERDAM • PARIS • SYDNEY • HAMBURG
STOCKHOLM • ATHENS • TOKYO • MILAN • MADRID
PRAGUE • WARSAW • BUDAPEST • AUCKLAND

ISBN 0-373-29137-X

THE LAW AND MISS HARDISSON

Visit us at www.eHarlequin.com

Printed in U.S.A.

Available from Harlequin Historicals and
LYNNA BANNING

Harlequin Historicals

To my aunt, Jean Banning Strickland

With special thanks to Suzanne Barrett, Ida Hills,
Norma Pulle and Leslie Yarnes Sugai.

Prologue

All he could remember was there were cherries on her hat. Bright, shiny, red cherries, nodding over her forehead. Nothing else penetrated the fog of pain and nausea while they'd loaded him into the stagecoach. He slumped into the corner seat and set himself to endure the thirty-mile trip across the eastern Oregon plains to Cedarville, where the driver claimed there was a doctor.

Early that morning he'd been full of beans and vinegar, anxious to get this job over with and head back to Texas, anxious for a meal he didn't have to cook over a fire he built himself. That ended when someone shot him off his horse and the gelding dragged him a quarter of a mile before he could get his boot out of the stirrup.

"He's probably broke some ribs and maybe busted his arm in a couple places," the stage driver had said. Someone sloshed whiskey down his throat and the cherry hat lady sniffed.

There were other passengers, but the one he vaguely remembered was the one who was dressed Eastern and acted mighty prim and proper. The driver suggested she might care to wait for another stage, but she gave him a frosty look and in a tone like flint said, "I am expected in Crazy Creek, and I intend to get there." After a pause, she added, "Is he more drunk, or more hurt?"

"Oh, Lordy, ma'am. He ain't a drinkin' man. But he shore is hurt. Somebody musta bushwacked him, cuz he's good with a gun, bein' a Texas Ranger, y'see. He ain't likely to lose a fair fight. He's hurt, sure enough."

"Very well. He is as anxious as I am to get to town. Why delay further?"

The driver grunted.

When the coach started up, his head slid forward against the siding. Then something soft and warm cushioned his cheek and he vaguely remembered a wet, cool cloth against his face and a not-to-be-denied voice saying crisply, "Drink this," and the burn of straight whiskey from a tilted bottle.

When they pulled into the dusty town, he remembered that she climbed out and started giving orders. "Watch his head. If the doctor is nearby, you men can carry him."

"Yes, ma'am," the driver said.

"Wait!" she commanded. "Should he have more whiskey if the pain gets worse?"

"We ain't got more, ma'am. Only had one bottle."

She looked up and down the dusty trail that passed for a street, pulled a bill from her reticule and handed it over. "Get whatever you think he might need, and bring me the change."

They manhandled him out of the coach and he thought dimly that his chest might explode with the pain. But the only thing he could recall clearly were the bright red cherries on her hat.

When he finally regained consciousness, he was on a bed in the corner of the doctor's office, trussed up in tape and bandages with one helluva headache.

Chapter One

Crazy Creek, Oregon
1883

Clayton Black drew rein at the top of the hill and gazed down at the secluded valley stretching below him. He sucked in some air, winced at the familiar pain in his rib cage and let his breath out easy. Two of his ribs were bruised, the doctor had said. One was cracked. He couldn't take a breath without being reminded.

He rubbed his injured arm as he gazed down at the creek twisting through the land. Bordered by gray-green willow and cottonwood trees, it lazily encircled the tidy town and then meandered off to the west.

He hurt enough that camping out another night

held little appeal, but still he hesitated. Crazy Creek looked too civilized to attract an outlaw like Brance Fortier, but you never knew. Maybe Fortier had passed through here. Maybe somebody had seen him, would remember which way he was headed. Not likely he'd stay long in a town as peaceful as this.

Clayton didn't plan to, either. Just the look of the place—trim picket fences, rosebushes in bloom, boardwalks on both sides of the streets—gave him the jitters. Too orderly. Too civilized.

He squinted under the wide brim of his hat. Newspaper office, mercantile, hotel, livery stable, barbershop, sheriff's office. A gleaming white church steeple drew his gaze and he groaned. It was one of those towns full of pious people and prayer meetings. A white steeple town.

Too much like his mother's meticulously kept plantation in Louisiana, and not enough like the dusty, ramshackle ranch in East Texas he and his father called home. Or had, before Fortier killed him.

A lump the size of a walnut swelled in his throat. *I'll get him, Pa. You just lie easy and don't worry.* If he got back alive, he vowed he'd plant a sweetbriar rosebush on the graves of his father and his sister.

Once more, Clayton directed his gaze on the little town curled in the lap of the green valley. The late morning sun poured down like honey. The landscape was so different from the dry, sagebrush-dotted desert he'd ridden over the past four days for a moment he thought the view might be a mirage, a glimpse of some lush emerald and gold paradise. Only thirty miles from Cedarville, but it looked like another planet.

He'd bet money it was Fortier who had winged him and then kicked in his ribs. All he remembered was the thump and sting of the bullet in his shoulder and waking up with his arm in a sling. Now, in addition to the warrant he carried for the outlaw, he had a personal score to settle. His crippled arm was his gun arm. It would be weeks, maybe months, before he could shoot straight.

He tossed back his chin-length black hair and ran his tongue over dry lips. He knew Fortier had passed this way; the outlaw's trail led straight toward town. He lifted the reins and stepped his horse back from the cliff edge. "C'mon, Rebel. Time to go."

Funny name, Crazy Creek. There was something he should remember about it, but he couldn't recall what. Since the shooting, there were still things he couldn't remember, but something about the place tugged at his insides. It was so pretty and serene it looked painted. Except for that boy down there, larruping through an alfalfa field after his dog, it hardly looked real.

He urged his mount forward, letting it pick its own way down the steep path. However out of place the trim little village made him feel, he'd have to ask around. If he was lucky, he'd pick up Fortier's trail on the other side of town.

And if he wasn't lucky...well, then, Fortier would shoot him in the back, like he'd shot Pa and Jannie, and that would be that. In some ways, it would be a relief.

Clayton's lips twitched into a lopsided smile. He knew only one thing for certain—he would capture his father's killer or die trying.

The look of the town below him, so settled, so civilized, made him nervous. Yeah, a white steeple town, full of people with refined manners and an extra helping of bigotry.

He pursed his mouth and tried to whistle. No way. He didn't belong here.

Hell, what was new about that? Being half Cherokee meant he didn't much belong anywhere.

"There," Irene murmured in satisfaction. She rearranged the in-work file on the large oak desk and glanced approvingly at her well-organized office. It looked much more tidy since she'd washed the front windows and painted the rough pine walls. The sheriff wouldn't mind. Besides, he was out of town.

Her office adjoined his, but he didn't own the building. Nate Cummings, the undertaker, did.

She'd paid Nate three months' rent in advance and the stocky gray-bearded man had let her do anything she wanted. She'd even spread a large oval braided rug over the plank floor. While Nate's watery blue eyes had widened, he had snapped his mouth shut and said nothing.

"Crazy Creek never had no lawyer before," Nate told her. She'd been famous ever since her first afternoon in town when she'd hung out the engraved metal sign she'd brought from the East and promptly got involved in that hostage standoff. Now her pending work file—actually the oval top from one of her hatboxes—overflowed with appointment requests. In the sheriff's absence, she noted with a flush of pride, people turned to her for advice. They had waited years to settle property boundary questions, draw up wills, have marriages and births recorded. Townsfolk streamed into her office like spawning salmon.

On impulse, she moved to the window. Oh, how good it was to be here in the West! She never wanted to see Philadelphia again. She'd had enough of wealthy clients suing other wealthy clients over some Thoroughbred's bloodlines. Real law—the constitutional rights she believed in with every fiber of her being—was needed in the West. Out here, the country was still growing. Back East, life—at least for her—had stopped when pneumonia took her father. After that, she couldn't wait to leave.

Irene's throat closed. She decided to busy herself dusting out her desk drawers. Settling herself on the hard oak swivel chair, she pulled open the bottom right-hand drawer and leaned over to inspect the contents. A dried-up bottle of Sanford's ink, two dusty cigars, and—

The door banged open. "Where's the sheriff?" a low, gravelly voice inquired.

"Gone," Irene said without looking up. "Is there something I can—"

"Gone where?"

Irene raised her gaze to the doorway and stopped breathing. A tall man stood before her, one arm in a black cloth sling, his leather vest coated with trail dust, his tanned face impassive. Steady gray eyes held hers. "Gone where?" he prompted.

Irene jerked to attention. "Gone, um, gone—" She couldn't think with him staring at her that way! "Gone…hunting!"

"Where's this I. P. Hardisson, then? Sign says he's a lawyer."

"He is. I mean, I am! I am I. P. Hardisson."

He looked her over for so long she felt tingles at the back of her neck. "Irene Pennfield Hardisson," she supplied. Something about the man unnerved her, but she managed to keep her voice steady. "Attorney-at-law," she added unnecessarily.

"Clayton Black, Texas Ranger." His eyes still rested on hers, but he didn't move. Tall and lean, he just stood and looked his fill.

"Mr. Black." Irene extended her hand.

He gave her fingers a quick, hard shake with his left hand, then stuffed his hand into his back pocket. "You ever hear of anyone by the name of Fortier?"

"Brance Fortier?"

"That's him. You know him?"

"N-not exactly."

"Where is he?"

"I—he was in jail when I arrived in Crazy Creek—"

"Jail!"

"Yes, but they released him."

"They what?" His eyes turned to cold steel.

"Well, I—he was accused of stealing a—"

"I'll bet," Clayton said in a dry voice. "Probably ran his own horse to death. So they let him go?"

It was more an accusation than a question. Irene's resolve stiffened. "A man," she pronounced in measured tones, "is presumed innocent until proven—"

"Horse-rocks!"

"Please let me finish."

Clayton took two long steps forward and leaned over her desk. "Okay," he said. "Finish."

She blinked. His face was so close to hers she could see the flush of anger on his high cheek-bones. Hair black as midnight swept his collar.

"—until proven guilty," she concluded.

"Yeah, I've heard that. But what I want with Fortier hasn't anything to do with horse-thievin', so where do I find him?"

"I have no idea where he went after the hostage exchange."

"Hostage exchange! Who was involved in that?"

"That you will have to ask the sheriff," she replied with a sniff. She didn't want to admit it was she who had negotiated the exchange. He looked mad enough as it was.

"Well now, I can't do that now, can I? Seein' as he's gone 'hunting.' Just what is he hunting, Miss Hardisson?"

Something about the man's deliberate, self-confident manner made her insides fluttery.

"I cannot say."

"Can't?" he pressed.

"Will not," she amended. She had no legal leg to stand on, and she knew it. She swept the crumbling cigars into the wastebasket beside her desk and tried to think. For some reason she didn't want to reveal to this man her role in Brance Fortier's release. She looked him in the eye and shook her head.

"You're obstructing justice, Miss Hardisson. I have a warrant for Fortier's arrest." With his good arm, he withdrew the paper from his inside vest pocket and unfolded it on her desk.

Irene scanned the document. "Murder! Oh, my."

"So you see, ma'am, you've gone and put your legal foot right in the middle of my job, and I suggest—"

"This is Oregon, not Texas," she enunciated with care. "Have you authority in Oregon?"

She prayed he would not challenge the point. She'd read law under her father in Pennsylvania; she hadn't been out West long enough to know Oregon law.

He ignored her question. "When did you see Fortier last?"

"A few days ago. I went over to the jail—"

"And released him," he finished for her. "I'll bet he lit out within ten minutes."

Irene drew in her breath and exhaled. "It was more like five minutes."

Clayton laughed out loud. "Brance Fortier's one of the old Cortina gang. I doubt he's within a hundred miles of this valley by now."

"I am quite sure he will be back within the week." She started to rise.

Clayton pinned her wrist to the desk. "Either you are a damn fool," he said quietly, "or you are a damn good liar."

Irene wrenched her hand free and stood up, breathing hard. "Mr. Black, if you will excuse me, I have business elsewhere. Good afternoon."

She slammed the desk drawer shut, yanked her black silk parasol from the china stand beside her desk and marched past him to the door.

He got there ahead of her.

"Stand aside, please," she ordered. She looked up at him with fire in her eyes. He noted they were an odd shade of green, and the mass of dark chestnut hair piled on top of her head seemed too heavy for the slim neck. The rest of her was pure woman. Small waist, gently flaring hips, skin like peach silk. The soft green dress clung to her upper torso in a way that made his mouth go dry, and her large, expressive eyes, framed by definite eyebrows and thick, black lashes, looked fearless.

He folded his good arm over his sling, content to block her way. She smelled good. Sweet and clean, like soap. He inclined his head toward her to get another whiff.

And then he spied something over her shoulder. Something she had forgotten in her fury. It sat on a glass-fronted bookcase behind the desk, and he hadn't seen it because he'd been focusing on those green eyes of hers.

Balls of fire, there couldn't be more than one creation like that in the entire country!

And there it was, right smack in front of him. That straw hat with the shiny red cherries on top.

Chapter Two

The parasol opened with a swish. Beneath the arch of black silk a pair of flashing eyes held his. "Why are you staring at me like that?"

"You're the lady on the stagecoach!" Clayton managed. "I recognize your hat."

The green eyes widened. "My hat?"

"Ma'am, I was badly wounded. As I recall, you got some whiskey for me, and for that I am eternally grate—"

"Whiskey!" She studied his face, then inspected the sling on his arm. Her face changed. "Oh, yes, I remember now."

"The doctor in Cedarville dug out the bullet and taped up my ribs. I'm obliged to you, Miss Hardisson."

Her dark brows drew into a frown. "It was Brance Fortier who shot you! That's why you want to find him, is it not? To settle the score?"

"Not exactly." Clayton shifted his weight, leaned his aching back against the closed door of her office. "To tell you the truth, ma'am, I don't know who shot me. Never saw him. Might've been Fortier. Might've been somebody else. Doesn't much matter, since I'm takin' Fortier back to Texas soon as I find him, to stand trial for murder."

"I am sorry, Mr. Black. Brance Fortier is not going anywhere until he is tried for horse theft here in Clackamas County."

She said it with such conviction Clayton gritted his teeth. *Why, why was he saddled with this annoyingly stubborn lady?* She sure didn't act as soft as she looked, small and fragile in green-sprigged muslin puffs and ribbons. She acted like she knew something he didn't, and it got under his skin. He needed to find out where Fortier had gone and get the hell out of this place! The town and everything in it—especially her—made him uneasy. All he wanted was Fortier and justice. Swift and efficient.

And Irene Hardisson knew which direction he was headed. He cleared his throat. "Miss Hardisson, I'm dead tired and hot and sweaty from near twenty hours in the saddle. If you don't mind, we'll continue this skirmish later."

She sent him a look that would fry bacon. "Well, I never!" Hands propped on her hips, she stood toe-to-toe with him.

Clayton stifled a groan, then spun on his heel

and headed for the door. "I need some answers. I'll be back after supper."

"I will not be in after supper," she snapped. "I will be at my home."

"Fine," he shot back. "Where do you live?"

"I did not mean for you to call, Mr. Black. I am not receiving. I meant—"

"At the hotel, then. Later. I'll probably pick up a poker game, see what I can find out."

With a nod in her direction, he bolted through the doorway and was gone.

Openmouthed, Irene listened to his boots clump down the boardwalk. She most certainly would *not* see him later! Their business, such as it was, had been completed. She had absolutely no wish to see Clayton Black ever again.

On the stagecoach she had not paid that much attention to the injured man they had loaded aboard other than to supply some pain-deadening whiskey. He had looked every bit the lowlife. Now, the man might be dusty and rumpled, but with his tanned, even features and straight, dark hair, she noted he was extraordinarily handsome. She nudged the awareness to the back of her mind. A moment ago he had stood there, assessing her with those cold gray eyes, and she had felt...well, intimidated.

So what if he is a lawman? A Texas Ranger, or so he said. That did not mean he was a gentleman.

"Gentlemen," she announced to her pile of waiting papers, "do not intimidate ladies."

She swept to the bookcase behind the desk and retrieved her straw hat. Decorated as it was with shiny red fruit, it had cost her four whole dollars at Whyte's in Philadelphia. She'd bought it because it reminded her of her father; he had adored cherries.

"And a poker-playing lawman at that," she muttered. "Papa always said that was the devil's game. That's why he taught me to play chess instead."

She pulled the door closed behind her, locked it with the key she dug out of her reticule, and headed down Park Street to her cottage.

Her spirits drooped. Another restless night with nothing to occupy her mind but how lonely she felt, so far away from everything familiar to her—the solid brick house she'd grown up in, her father's library of books, her father himself, dead these past four months.

On the surface, she maintained the cool, controlled manner that had been bred into her, but inside, when she was alone, she had to face her real feelings. Her soul ached at the loss of her father. She would never see his dear, bewhiskered face again.

Her shoulders sagged. She was two thousand miles from the cobblestone streets of Philadelphia, the comfortable, welcoming home she'd always known. She longed to be there now, longed to let Nora help her out of her stays and petticoats, draw her a bath, bring supper on a tray. For all the years she could remember, the plump housekeeper had loved her and taken care of her, just like a mother. Oh, why had she ever left?

Because it was not enough, a voice inside reminded. *You wanted to make your own way, be a part of the new Western frontier.*

Well, now she was part of it, God help her! She supposed men like Clayton Black went with the territory. Men who hunted other men. Men who intimidated women. Men who frequented smoke-filled rooms playing…poker.

It was only a game, wasn't it? Why had Father been so against it?

She loved games, excelled at them. Loved the feeling of control she gained when she mastered the rules. She guessed her joy in such activity was an antidote to losing her mother when she was four, and the confusion that overwhelmed her later when her father began to fail.

She had studied law not only to uphold the name of the Hardisson law firm but because it offered her a kind of emotional security. She could not predict life or death, but with intelligence and knowledge of the rules, she *could* dictate the outcome of a trial. Or a game.

The thought pulled at her as she turned the corner across from the town square and sped toward the white frame house that was now hers. Inside was safety and warmth. Predictability. After her encounter with Clayton Black, she felt more than the usual need for such things.

"But at least I had the last word," she announced to her empty front parlor. She halted in front of four rolls of rose-sprigged wallpaper she'd left leaning against the stepladder. "Or did I?"

She could not remember. When he had looked at her, under her corset her heart began to hammer like a piston and her thoughts flew up and away like so many dandelion puffs.

She smoothed her palm over the carved oak banister in the hall and stepped with exaggerated dignity onto the first stair. "I am becoming a notional old maid with a silly brain that goes into flutters over a Texas Ranger's smile! Well, I will have none of *that,* thank you. None whatsoever!" She reached the top landing and marched to her bedroom door.

Inside, the golden afternoon light poured in the open window, bringing the scent of roses and Mrs. Gerstein's honeysuckle vine from the neighboring yard. Irene shut her eyes. *Papa is gone.*

She opened her eyes and spoke aloud to the windowpane. "And he is never coming back."

* * *

"Cut the cards, mister?"

Clayton reached out his good arm and split the deck. He'd played seven hands, won the pot after the last one, and now his mind wandered away from the game while the dealer slapped cards down onto the scarred oak table.

Sweat crawled down his back. He felt off balance. He'd unpinned the badge on his vest to forestall questions, had been invited to join the game with no inquiries. He wondered if the five men gathered around the table would be as friendly if they knew he was a Texas Ranger. If they knew he was after information, they might clam up.

He didn't belong here. If they knew he was half Cherokee, he wouldn't even be allowed in. The sign in the hotel lobby said No Indians. He longed to get up and leave, but it was too early to break up the game. He hadn't learned a damn thing about Fortier so far. Maybe he was sitting at the wrong campfire.

Irene Hardisson knew more than she was telling, he could feel it in his gut. It was her he had to talk to.

She sure hadn't had much to say to him this afternoon!

A grin threatened to crack his dry lips. Man, she had a temper. She was starched stiff as a corset stay!

He shifted in his chair. Even after two whiskeys, his shoulder hurt and his ribs still ached. A soft bed with clean sheets beckoned upstairs—why not wait till morning to talk to the lady lawyer?

Yeah, Clayton, mi amigo. *Why not?*

Because she smelled good. And she looked soft and frilly and her dark hair shone like firelight licking coals, and...she smelled good. Like a woman.

And because he was hungry for something he couldn't even begin to name. Someone to talk to. Somewhere to belong.

Just for tonight. Tomorrow he'd head out and try to pick up Fortier's trail. It made him nervous to stay in one place too long. But tonight...tonight he wished—

"Mr. Black?"

In an instant, the entire table of men rose to their feet. Clayton's cards slipped from his hand and scattered, most of them faceup. Without turning his head, he knew who it was. In a town like this, men stood up when a lady entered a room.

He stood up, too, removing his hat as he did so, just like his momma had taught him.

"Miss Hardisson."

"I have come to apologize," she said in a low voice.

With his left hand, he grasped her elbow and turned her toward the entrance. "You shouldn't be in here, this is a—"

"I know what it is. A card room."

"The lady is welcome to stay," one of the men offered.

"No, thank you," came her crisp reply. "I came only to speak to Mr. Black about...a certain matter."

Clayton steered her through the doorway and into the hotel foyer, then turned her to face him. "About Brance Fortier?"

The dark lashes descended, but not before he saw that her eyes looked odd. Uncertain.

"Miss Hardisson," he prompted. "About Fortier?"

"About poker." She blurted the words and shut her lips tight.

"What?" he said, louder than he intended.

"Poker," she repeated. "I want you to teach me how to play poker."

Clayton released her arm and took a step backward. "Are you crazy? Ladies don't play poker!"

"Why not? I am skilled at hearts and baccarat. Why not poker?"

He searched for a reply. "It's...complicated."

"I am quite intelligent. I want to learn."

"Well, I'll be—what the hell *for?*" His voice came out so loud the drowsing hotel clerk jerked awake. "What the hell for?" he said more softly.

Her face changed. "I have my reasons."

Clayton frowned. In the space of a few seconds,

her expression had gone from hopeful to determined and back to hopeful. It didn't make any sense.

They looked at each other in silence. "You want—need—something from me," she said at last. "And I want something from you."

He knew she didn't mean it the way it sounded, but his heart leaped anyway. The word "want" on her tongue made his throat go dry.

"And that is?"

"Teach me."

Under his jeans, Clayton felt his groin tighten. "To play poker," he said.

"Yes."

"Why should I?"

"Because," she said, her voice even, her face studiedly calm, "I can make it worth your while."

His heartbeat stuttered. She was an innocent, so naive she didn't know how suggestive her words were, especially to a starving man. He cleared his throat and worked to keep his voice steady. "Just what are you prepared to offer?"

Irene cocked her head. "Information. About Brance Fortier."

He knew he was gaping at her. Twice he had to remind himself to close his mouth. Disappointment that her bargaining chip was limited to information warred with curiosity about what she knew.

"It's a deal."

"Very well. Shall we commence here, in the hotel?"

"Too public, you bein' a lady and all. You live in town, I reckon. How about your place?"

"That would not be at all proper, I'm afraid. We would have no chaperon."

Chaperon! She talks about making it worth my while and then... Right. She's offering information. Just information.

"What about your law office?"

She considered his suggestion, then nodded. "I'll fetch a pot of coffee."

"I'll bring a deck of cards." *And all the restraint I can muster.* Damn, but she looked pretty when she smiled. Didn't do it very often, but it was like the sun in summer when she did.

She turned away and stepped daintily toward the hotel entrance, then pivoted toward him. "I've been waiting for this for years, Mr. Black. I know I'm going to enjoy it!"

Clayton groaned and watched her ruffled backside sway down the hotel steps and up the street.

Hell's fireballs! He couldn't have resisted following her if he was made out of solid granite and welded to the floor!

Chapter Three

Irene unlocked the door to her office and set the coffee tray from the Maybud Hotel on the table just inside the entrance while she lit the single kerosene lamp. In the soft glow of light she whisked her desk clear of her appointment calendar and the stack of work in her hatbox, then retrieved the enamelware pot. Advancing to set the tray on her desk, a thought struck her.

Her mother would spin in her grave at the prospect of entertaining a man late at night, unchaperoned, without a single thought to propriety! And Nora—she'd best not think about what Nora would say. Why, oh why had she suggested it?

Because you are restless and lonely. She needed to do something, keep busy. And when he'd mentioned poker…

She couldn't abide knitting, or needlework of any kind for that matter. It gave her a terrible headache. But she did love games. Learning a new one would give her something to do, something to think about besides how much she missed Papa. In fact, she thought with an inward smile, were he acquainted with the circumstances, her father would surely advise her to seize the opportunity!

She released a long sigh. Papa always was a very practical man.

Clayton stepped through the open door, noiseless as a cat. "Good evening, Miss Hardisson." He removed his wide-brimmed gray hat and hung it on the peg just inside the door.

Irene sank onto her desk chair. Then she straightened her spine and sent a sideways glance at him as he folded his long body into the chair across from her. He held her gaze, amusement dancing in his eyes.

Quelling the tiny flutter in her belly, she leaned toward him. "Would you," she said in a voice not quite her own, "please explain the rules of the game?"

Clayton leaned back against the oak chair frame and studied the young woman across from him. She'd brought a whole pot of hot coffee from the hotel dining room, and he appreciated that. But the rest of it didn't make much sense.

She looked too citified to be sitting here in an Oregon frontier law office, even one with whitewashed walls and lace curtains at the window. She spoke and moved like a lady—an educated lady at that—but as he explained the game of five-card draw poker, she looked more and more like a little girl reveling in wide-eyed fascination over a new toy. Her eyes sparkled as he described the suits, the various hands and their relative value, how to deal and bet and call.

Most surprising of all, the lady lawyer who had all the answers this afternoon said not one word. She just listened with that intent look of concentration on her face, the cherries on her hat bobbing when she nodded. She never asked a question. She never asked him to repeat anything. Most of it must be over her head, and he was amused and not a little admiring of her focus on the complicated game.

At the conclusion of his instructions, she smiled up at him. "Do let's play a round!"

"Play a hand," he corrected.

"Very well, a hand, then. May we?" She laced her fingers together under her chin and Clayton had to chuckle. She looked like a hungry urchin eyeing a pan of hot biscuits. This was more than interesting—it was unbelievable!

He tried not to smile at her delight. "Deal the cards," he ordered.

She shuffled the deck awkwardly, presented them for cutting, and dealt out five cards each. "What shall we use for betting?"

Clayton blinked. Ladies didn't gamble. Somehow he figured she'd prefer to play without betting. On the other hand, nothing much would surprise him at this point. He was already nonplussed by a thing or two about this particular lady. With a jolt he realized he had forgotten he was playing for information about Brance Fortier. Bets it would be.

"We could use matches," she suggested.

"Don't have enough."

She raised her eyes to his. "What about dried beans?"

"Don't know many lawyers who keep a stash of dried beans around. You got some?"

"Well, no. I've been taking my meals at the hotel until my stove is delivered."

"Not beans, then, it looks like."

"There must be *something* we could bet!"

He liked the way she didn't give up on an idea right away. She had a most unladylike amount of grit, and he liked that, too. In fact, he mused as he watched her eyes widen at the cards in her hand, he found himself downright content in her company. He hadn't felt comfortable around a woman since…

The warning bell went off in his head just as she looked up. *Take one fine-looking female and stir in a healthy dose of interest and you've got trouble.* Big trouble. The kind he swore never to risk again.

He had to get this over with and get out of here. If her mind was so set on playing poker, he'd use that to his advantage.

"This might seem a little unusual, ma'am, but once we had a Mexican foreman and an Indian wrangler on the ranch. They were usually on opposite sides in the skirmishes the Mexicans and the Comanches got into in Texas, so when they played cards, they bet 'truths.'"

"Truths? How do you mean?"

"We called it Truth Poker."

Her eyes lit up. "You mean the winner could ask a question and the loser had to answer it?"

"Yep. You can see why bets never got very high."

She leaned across the desk. "But it sounds like such fun! Perhaps we could do the same?"

Clayton regarded her with satisfaction. "You serious?"

"Of course I'm serious! Hardissons do not mince words when it comes to the truth—it's an immutable constant in a world of turmoil and change. It is an obligation of honor to seek it out. Truth," she reiterated, "is sacred!"

She straightened her shoulders. He watched the soft green dress pull over her breasts. She looked straight into his eyes and Clayton felt his gut tighten. Her dress was the exact shade of her eyes, a clear, sea green with startling flecks of amber.

"Truth," he enunciated carefully over a throat gone dry, "is relative."

Her head came up. "Truth is what is true." The cherries waved like miniature boats on a stormy ocean.

"Either way, ma'am, it's a matter of honor. If we agree to this kind of bet, neither of us can lie."

"Of course not!" she agreed with a smart little nod of her head. "That's what will make it interesting. Your move, I believe?"

All at once Clayton thought of a hundred reasons why he shouldn't be doing this. It was one thing for Luis and White Owl to barter information. As a matter of fact it made the bunkhouse card games unbeatable entertainment—you never knew what you were going to hear.

But what the hell was *he* doing, gambling with *his* secrets? Sweat gathered at the base of his neck, and not because of the oppressive heat in the small room. For another, more disturbing reason.

The night air hung heavy and still, as if waiting for something. A thundershower, maybe. Through the door she'd purposely propped open he smelled the dust, the faint scent of sagebrush, smoke from some strolling ranch hand's hand-rolled cigarette. If he had the sense God gave an ant, he'd call a halt to the poker lesson and walk this lady safely back to her residence.

Without conscious thought, his lips opened. "I'll take one card."

She slapped it down and he glanced at it, suppressing a smile. He needn't worry. It would be over soon. He'd win this hand easily. In fact, she was so green he'd win every game and that prospect caught his interest. He'd worm out of her what she was hiding about Fortier in three hands. Four at the most.

"I'll bet one question." He watched her face.

She was obviously pretty smart. He wanted to see what she'd do when she lost her wager and he began to probe.

What occurred to him next sent a current of excitement through his brain.

Under the guise of the poker game, he could ask her anything he wanted, find out *her* secrets. That intrigued him almost as much as Fortier's whereabouts.

Again the warning whisper in his brain. *If you weren't curious about her in the first place, you wouldn't give two figs who won the game.*

But he *was* curious. Interested. Drawn to her, even.

All of it. Clayton sighed as she peeled two cards off the top of the deck and slid them into her hand. Her eyelids flicked down, then up. "Call."

He laid his cards faceup on the desk. "Two pair, kings and jacks."

"Full home," she replied in a matter-of-fact voice. "Three queens and a pair of fives."

Clayton stared at the cards. "Full *house*," he mumbled. "Hellfire, a full house!"

"Excuse me, yes—a full house." She glowed with triumph, her cheeks rosy, her green eyes dancing.

"And now, for my question." The smile she sent him made his head spin.

"Yeah?" It was all he could think of to say.

The lady with the cherries on her hat cocked her head. "Tell me, then, Mr. Black. What exactly are you hiding about Brance Fortier?"

Clayton jerked. "Why do you think *I'm* hiding something?"

"I just do. I sense it. When you talked about him this afternoon, you stared at the floor. Only the floor. Yet when you spoke of other things, you looked directly at me."

"I did, did I?"

"You did."

"You're pretty observant," he grumbled.

"I am extremely observant, yes," she agreed, her voice low. "And you owe me a truthful answer. What really happened in Texas that you should come all the way to Oregon to settle it?"

Lord, he was trapped. Hoisted in his own net. He closed his eyes.

He didn't know whether he could tell her. He

was honor-bound to speak the truth, but he wasn't sure he could get the words out. Wasn't sure he could live with himself if he heard his voice say out loud what had really occurred.

"Mr. Black?" she reminded. "A pledge is a pledge. I'm waiting."

"You bring any whiskey for the coffee?"

Her eyes grew round. "No."

Clayton groaned.

"But I could get some," she added quickly. "From the establishment across the street."

"Forget it. I don't want you going into a saloon. I'll do without it."

She waited. Over the sound of their breathing in the soft night air came the scrape of crickets and a tinny piano playing an old song he used to like. "Lorena."

All at once he couldn't breathe. He'd have to speak of it, maybe not tell all of it, but enough to satisfy the game of honor he'd so foolishly started. *God in heaven,* he prayed. He wasn't sure he could do even that much.

"Okay, Miss Hardisson. Listen up."

The penetrating green eyes traveled over him as if he were a bug caught under a magnifying glass. He resisted the urge to stand up and smooth back his hair for inspection.

Irene focused her attention on the cords that stood out on Clayton Black's tanned neck. She had him now. But for some reason her feeling of triumph faded as she watched him lick his lips over and over. Whatever he had kept hidden, it was hard for him to speak of.

Suddenly she was sorry she had asked that particular question. His obvious pain made her throat ache.

"Pa—my father—was Josh Black. A Ranger, like me. Last spring he tracked some of Juan Cortina's old gang over the border into Louisiana, and I went with him. Turned out my mother's half brother was one of them. We caught up with him at my mother's place near New Orleans."

Clayton angled his body away from her, spoke with his face turned toward the window. "We split up to make the capture, and Dad moved off a ways to draw Fortier's fire away from me. When he yelled for me to move in, Fortier spun around and shot him. I—"

He stopped and pressed his lips into a straight line. "I should have gotten a bullet into the bastard, but I wasn't fast enough."

His long fingers closed into fists. "I tried to get to Dad, but Fortier came toward me and then my kid sister ran out of the house. Fortier grabbed her and put a revolver to the back of her neck. Jannie kept looking at me, kind of smiling, even though I could see she was scared. 'You'll do the right thing, Clay,' she said."

A horrible sense of foreboding settled over Irene. She reached out one hand to stop him.

"Fortier saw me coming and he put a bullet into me to stop me. Just missed killing me. Then he dragged Jannie off behind the stable and..." He sucked in a harsh breath.

Irene pressed her fist against her mouth. No more. She could not stand to hear more.

"By the time I reached her, he'd shot her, too."

"Oh, I am so sorry," she whispered. "So sorry to have asked you to speak of it. I beg your forgiveness, Mr. Black."

He leveled his gaze on her, his gray eyes unfathomable. "Luck of the draw, I guess."

She racked her brain for what to say. "I—of course you would prefer not to play any more poker."

His lips formed a one-sided smile. "Who says so? Can't say I enjoyed losing the first hand, but the game's not over, Miss Hardisson. Not by a long shot. You owe me a chance to recoup my loss, so to speak."

"Oh. Well, I..." She shuffled the cards to hide her confusion. She definitely did not wish to admit her part in freeing Fortier. But if what Clayton Black said was true, if Brance Fortier was a murderer... She didn't know what to do.

On the other hand, she would like to find out all she could about the enigmatic man sitting across from her. One way to do that was to win another hand of poker. But could she really *do* that?

Of course she could! It was a simple matter of keeping her head and hiding her feelings. Goodness knows, after twenty-five years in straitlaced Philadelphia society, she was an expert at that!

Clayton cut the deck and she dealt another hand, gathered up her cards and suppressed a gasp. Ace, king, queen of diamonds. Quickly she discarded the two unrelated cards. She needed a jack and a ten, and she put all her concentration on those numbers.

Clayton grunted. "I'll hold."

She pressed two cards facedown on the desk, then set the deck aside and peeked at her hand.

Nothing. Not even two of a kind. She'd have to bluff. She could feel his eyes studying her, and she tried to keep her face expressionless. "I bet one question."

"Raise you one."

"You mean if I win, I may ask *two* questions?"

"That's right. And if you fold—"

"Oh, I won't fold," she said with an assurance she did not feel. Desperately she hoped he would be taken in by her pretense and would toss in his cards first. That way, she need never show her worthless hand and she would win another—no, two—more questions. It was worth a try.

"Meet my bet or fold," he instructed.

"Very well." It occurred to her that *he* might be bluffing as well. She hoped so. That way she might save face. She watched as he laid his cards faceup on the barrel.

"Pair of kings," he said in a low voice.

"Oh. I—well, I..." With a sigh she laid down her cards. "You win."

"Damn right," he drawled. "Now you get to give *me* some answers."

Chapter Four

Irene flinched. She looked up into Clayton Black's hard, steady gaze and her heart gave a little skip. Such cool, calculating eyes, and that knowing expression, as if he could see into her thoughts. She steeled herself to admit as little as possible but still forfeit the "truth" he'd won.

Clayton's lips opened. "Okay, here's my first question. Why are you unmarried?"

"What?" The breath caught in her lungs. She expected him to ask about Fortier, not her.

"You heard me. I figure you're about twenty-five. If I remember correctly, most society ladies back East have a brood of younguns by that age. How come you don't?"

"I'm twenty-six," she said quickly. "I've been...busy."

"Busy," he repeated. "Busy being a lawyer instead of a woman, is that it?" He sat back, considering. "Sorry, but I don't buy that. Nobody with a functioning blood supply is that busy. Now, you owe me the truth, so let's hear it."

Irene bit her lower lip. What insolence! He had no right to ask such a thing. No man with any manners would pose such a question.

"Don't you want to know about Brance For—"

"Nope. At least not yet. I figure I've got plenty of time for that." He folded his arms across his chest and waited.

You lost the bet, a voice reminded. *Now you must pay up.*

"Oh, all right," she blurted. "My mother died when I was four, and I resolved I would never… entertain any gentlemen callers. I made a promise on her grave to devote my life to taking care of Papa."

His eyes flickered, then softened. "How'd she die?"

Irene swallowed. "She was out riding. The horse refused a jump and threw her. Her neck was broken." She drew in a breath to steady her nerves. "Why would you want to know such a thing?"

Clayton gave her a long, assessing look. "Don't know, exactly. Just wonder what a pretty woman's doing in a little picture-book town like Crazy Creek. Why she'd come out West to be a lawyer. It isn't for money, I knew that right off. Your dress and that hat say you don't need money. So why?"

Irene opened her mouth, then closed it. "I assume that is your second question?"

He nodded.

She thought for a moment. True, she did not need money. But she did need…something. Freedom, maybe. A new start in life. *Something.* However, she wasn't about to admit this to Clayton Black. No sirree. He would laugh at her.

But, she reminded herself, she had to answer truthfully. He had done so, at some expense; it was a matter of honor.

"I have never been completely on my own before," she confessed.

"Thought so," Clayton said, his voice quiet.

Her head came up. "You what? I assure you, Mr. Black, I am a very capable attorney."

"Thought that, too," he responded. "Just curious is all."

"About what, exactly?" Her tone sounded extra prim, even to her.

"About you."

"Me! Why would you want to know—"

He chuckled. "To find that out, you're gonna have to win another hand."

Another hand? Her pulse jumped. Actually, she enjoyed the game—it was the forfeited truths that bothered her. Answering his question made her uneasy, as if she were filled with sand and telling things about herself allowed some of her insides to leak away. She wondered if he felt the same way.

She should end this charade right this minute. Return to her cottage and read or…do something. Anything. Even hang wallpaper.

Her brain told her it was just a card game, a harmless pastime. Her heart told her something else—that it was dangerous. The more he unearthed about her, the more vulnerable she felt.

And that, she realized all at once, was how she had grown up—protecting herself from the real world of loss and pain by keeping everything hidden inside herself.

She felt dazed. Some sort of tension was building between herself and Clayton Black. Not as an opponent, but as a man.

Against her better judgment, Irene gathered up the deck and reshuffled it. She laid out five fresh cards for each of them and watched his capable fingers fold themselves around his hand.

"You know," he said as she gathered up her own cards, "When I find Fortier, I just might kill him." The words he heard himself utter sent a cold fist of surprise into his gut. He'd never shot a man in cold blood. Never even considered it.

"I don't believe so, Mr. Black. For one thing, you'd hang for murder."

"Tell the truth, sometimes I kinda figure on that. I don't know how I'll feel living and remembering what Fortier did to Pa and Jannie. Dangling at the end of a rope would be quick and easy.''

Irene heard his words through a jumble of her own thoughts. The man had given up hope. He would throw his life away because he was desperately lost, alienated from himself. Alone. She knew how he felt, knew the hurt, the helpless fury that came with the loss of someone you loved. They had both come to Crazy Creek on the same quest— to find a reason for living.

A little flutter of pleasurable apprehension laced across her belly. She wondered about him. She wanted to know…all kinds of things. She had to win the next hand!

Which she did. Her three nines beat his pair of jacks.

''Now for my question, Mr. Black.'' She paused to phrase it with gentility. ''What is the reason for your curiosity regarding my person?''

His gray eyes regarded her with studied detachment. ''The truth?''

She nodded. ''The truth.''

''Well, now there's different levels of truth.''

''I want to hear them all,'' Irene heard herself say.

''All right, then. On one level, I'd say it's because you don't 'fit' out here, and things—people—that don't fit kinda make my nose twitch.''

"It is true, I do not fit. I come from Philadelphia."

"And on another level I'd say because you're the best-looking thing in this town and I've got a bit of time to admire it and be a tad curious."

"Oh. Oh!"

"And at bottom, I guess you could say I haven't had a woman in more than a year and I just wondered about you, the way a man wonders about a woman."

"Mr. Black!" Irene jumped to her feet.

He lifted his hands from the desk and slowly got to his feet. "Miss Hardisson," he echoed. "I warned you about this game. Truth is what we *think* we want to hear. Most times the real truth is unwelcome or shocking or—like right now— damned impolite. My apologies for offending you."

Irene hesitated. She wasn't offended, not deep inside. She was thrilled right down to her toes! He was a man—all man, from his broad shoulders to his tooled leather boots—and he had those kinds of thoughts about *her?* Something turned over inside her chest.

"I accept your apology, Mr. Black." Her sentence came out a bit breathily, and she cringed in the silence. She couldn't let him see how pleased she was by his admission. No man had ever uttered such stirring words to her! Back in Philadelphia, young men spoke ridiculously flowery phrases. But *Miss Hardisson, I have long admired you from afar* just didn't measure up to this Western man's blunt talk.

She loved it!

Heavens to Betsy, what was wrong with her?

Clayton stepped around the desk and took her elbow. "That's probably enough poker for one evening. I'll escort you home."

"Mr. Black, you needn't—"

His fingers tightened on her arm. "Clay," he said. "And I do need."

He blew out the lamp and walked her out the door.

At the bottom of her porch steps he released her elbow. "Good night, Miss Hardisson."

She could not utter one single word. Everything about him pulled at her senses, his steady gray eyes, the squint lines etched at the corners, the dark, silky-looking hair that brushed his shoulders. She felt slightly dizzy in his presence.

She unlocked her door and on unsteady legs found her way upstairs to her bedroom. For an hour she sat staring out the open window, breathing in the warm, honeysuckle-scented air and feeling more lonely than ever before in her life.

Clayton. An unusual name. She'd ask him about it the next time they played poker.

* * *

Irene wakened when the sun was high and hot and the cackle of Mr. Gerstein's chickens floated from the neighboring yard, punctuated by the snip-snip of his wife's flower clippers. She lay still, listening.

A horse clopped by, pulling a rattletrap wagon. In its wake rose the scent of warm dust. Lulled by the sounds and smells, she offered up a short prayer of thanks to God for bringing her safely across the plains to this peaceful place.

Children's voices echoed from the path winding past her house to Schoolhouse Hill. When the bell began to clang, the voices gradually faded into silence.

Irene sat up. Heavens, it was nine o'clock! She had Mrs. Madsen's letter to answer and Arlen Svenson's will to draft! Hurriedly she splashed water from the china basin over her face and neck and dressed in a royal-blue sateen work skirt and high-necked white shirtwaist trimmed with lace. Arranging her hair in a loose bun on top of her head, she secured her straw hat in place with a pearl-tipped hat pin and descended the stairs.

Except for her footsteps on the wooden staircase, the house was quiet. It still smelled faintly of paint and wallpaper paste, but even in its unfurnished state, it felt like home. *Her* home.

Her furniture—inherited along with the Philadelphia house where she and her father had lived until death took him—would arrive in early August, along with Nora. At the moment she didn't miss either the housekeeper or her furniture.

She had selected only the most cherished pieces to ship west—the chiffonier from her mother's bedroom, her father's polished walnut rolltop desk, the embossed silver umbrella stand, Great-Aunt Emily's gold-bordered Haviland china, the Oriental carpets in her father's study, and the carved four-poster bed he slept in. The rest she had directed Nora to sell. She could purchase new settees and tables and chairs in Portland, seventy miles away.

In the meantime, she would manage. She much preferred a bedroll on her very own hardwood floor to Mrs. Bauer's boardinghouse across the street.

True, she was lonely, but not for her housekeeper. She still grieved over her father's loss, but she vowed she would not allow thoughts of missing him to spoil this brand-new, beautifully clear day.

In fact, she felt so full of energy she thought she might pop. First, breakfast at the Maybud Hotel dining room, and then…she rubbed her hands together relishing the prospect. Then she would finish up her letters and wallpaper the front parlor!

She could hardly believe she was here in this lovely little town, settled in a pretty white cottage on Park Street. She tried to suppress a smile, but it grew and grew, no matter what.

A whole month without Nora! She did miss the housekeeper, but now that she was here, on her own, she reveled in her newfound freedom. She could eat when she wished, give her own hair the required hundred brush strokes every night, brew her own afternoon tea, and even make the scones she was so fond of—once her stove arrived.

She could get along without the housekeeper for a month, surely. Besides, Nora had plenty to occupy her what with closing out a three-story house crammed with the belongings of four generations of Hardissons and Pennfields. Nora would have plenty of time, now that her father was gone.

She seized her parasol from the oversize vase in the corner and swung open the front door. Perhaps she would have enough of the flower-sprigged wallpaper left over to—

"Mornin', Miss Hardisson," a rich voice drawled. Clayton Black rose from the top porch step and tipped his hat.

"Mr. Black! What are you doing here at this hour?"

"Waitin' for you. Information. And breakfast, in that order."

"Breakfast!" Her stomach rumbled annoyingly, as if to reinforce the thought. "You'll get no breakfast here, I assure you."

"Thought not. You said you eat at the hotel."

Irene blinked. "And so?"

"So, I've got a notion to accompany you, if you don't mind."

Irene pointed the tip of her parasol at the sky and released the catch. "As a matter of fact, I do mind."

The mere sight of the man on her front porch chased away her appetite.

The ruffled silk dome opened in an arc over her head, and for one insane moment she gazed up at the metal ribs and wondered if what she had just uttered was true. The thought of Clayton Black looking at her across a table made her toes tingle. What *was* it about the man she found so unnerving?

She decided she didn't want to know. "I prefer to eat alone. I think about my schedule for the day, and often plan—"

"Schedule!"

"—tomorrow's schedule as well. Today being Friday, Saturday, too, will be allocated to productive activity."

"Productive activ—? Good gravy!"

She swept on, undeterred by his interruption. "And of course Sunday is the Lord's Day, and I shall rest."

"I should damn well think so. Don't you ever take any time for fun?"

"Fun?" She gave him a blank look. "You mean as in frivolity? The answer is no. My profession is my satisfaction in life. 'Fun,' as you put it, is for—"

"Normal people," Clayton interjected. "Ma'am, you'll forgive me for sayin' so, but you're in sorry shape." He advanced a step toward her and captured the hand holding the parasol. "Now just come along quiet-like, and we'll work this all out at breakfast. I'm half-starved. Another thirty minutes on your porch and I'd 'a taken a bite outta my hat, so hurry it up."

Irene stared up at him. "I'm not going anywhere with you," she announced. She planted her black laced-up walking shoes flat on the porch planking.

"Sure y'are." Clayton ran his forefinger over the hand clutching the parasol. "I notice you like to make wagers, Miss Hardisson. I'm bettin' you'll follow me when I tell you what I found out this morning." He stepped back.

Irene took a hesitant step forward. "What?" she demanded.

"Good girl," Clayton murmured. He stepped back again.

She followed him. "What did you find out?"

He did not reply. Instead, he slid his left arm under hers and drew her forward, down the porch steps and along Park Street.

Nelda Gerstein lifted her wicker flower basket

in greeting as they passed. "Lovely morning," she
sang.

Clayton nodded at the sweet-faced older woman
and touched his hat brim. "That it is, ma'am."

"A bit hot for July, but then my Thomas always
says…" Her voice receded as they moved down
the board sidewalk.

"Mr. Black," Irene huffed as he hurried her
along. "Just what do you think you're doing?"

"I'm takin' you to breakfast, Miss Hardisson."
His fingers wrapped over hers on the parasol handle as he guided her across the street toward the
hotel. Irene found it difficult to breathe normally
with his hard, warm hand on hers.

"And then—" he paused while they ascended
the three wide wooden steps at the hotel entrance
"—we're goin' on a picnic."

"Picnic! Right after breakfast? What on earth
for?"

"Reconnaissance," he said quietly. "You can
ride, can't you?"

"Most certainly I can ride." She closed the parasol with a snap. "I was named equestrienne of
the—"

"Good." He propelled her into the dining room,
selected a table by the front window and pulled
back her chair. "We'll have ham and eggs, over
easy," he said to the waitress. "And half-a-dozen
cold chicken sandwiches. For lunch," he added.

Irene bristled. "Now just one minute."

"Certainly, sir," the waitress breathed. She stood stock-still for a moment, staring at Irene, then she bobbed an awkward curtsy.

Clayton chuckled.

"I prefer to order my own meals," Irene hissed across the table. She turned to the wide-eyed girl. "I would like ham and two eggs, over easy."

He laughed out loud.

"And some tea, if you please." She worked to keep her voice even, but in spite of her efforts it rose alarmingly. The man was maddening. Overbearing. He acted as if he owned the hotel, the town—even her! Well, she'd soon set him straight on that score.

But you like it a little, don't you? a voice nagged. *Perhaps even more than a little?*

She most certainly did not!

Liar.

Clayton studied her face. "You look kinda funny, Miss Hardisson. Something wrong?"

Everything was wrong, she thought in exasperation. *Except for one thing,* the voice countered. *Him. You feel alive when he's near.*

"Nothing is wrong," she lied. "I am not accustomed to frittering away a perfectly good workday on picnics and such nonsense."

He nodded. "That figures."

"Consequently, I have no intention of accompanying you anywhere, much less on horseback." She flipped the white linen napkin open and settled it across her lap.

"I'll hire a buggy instead." His voice was calm, without the slightest inflection. His nonchalance made Irene clench her hands.

"No buggy," she enunciated clearly. "No horse. And no picnic." She dumped two heaping spoonfuls of sugar into her tea before she realized what she was doing.

Clayton signaled the waitress. "Better make it a dozen sandwiches. The lady will have quite an appetite."

The girl giggled. "Certainly, sir."

Irene gritted her teeth. "I will have no appetite whatsoever."

He tilted his chair back and gazed at her. "I think you will." Amusement and something else colored his voice, along with an undercurrent of steely determination that made her apprehensive.

"For one thing, with no buggy and no horse, that leaves us on foot." He tipped his chair forward. "I know from experience that walkin' works up a powerful hunger."

"Never!"

"Right after breakfast," he contradicted.

Irene squirmed on the straight-backed dining

chair. "What makes you think I would even consider—"

"Because, Miss Hardisson, you still haven't told me what I need to know, and I'm gettin' itchy. Now I don't hold with using force—" he looked deep into her eyes "—but the way I figure it, you owe me some information, so I'm gonna make you a proposition."

Her eyes flashed in alarm. "Mr. Black!" Her tone made him think of a mid-January Texas frost. She'd mistaken his meaning.

Clayton swallowed to wet his throat. "You ever see a chess match?"

"Why no, but—"

"Well then, here's the bargain. These two foreign fellas, Russians, I think, are playing chess over in Parker's Meadow. I'll take you to watch the match, and you'll give me what I'm after." He gulped. *Balls of fire, what was wrong with his tongue?*

She looked at him as if his ears were screwed on backward. For a long, long minute, she didn't say a word. He tried to read her thoughts, but she met his gaze with carefully expressionless eyes. She'd make a good poker player. He couldn't tell jack squat about what she was thinking.

He knew it was a long shot. She might have no interest in the game, much less stamina for an entire match, which could extend over the better part of a day. But she liked games, didn't she? She liked challenges. He'd wager she didn't know a thing about chess, but maybe she'd last long enough to let down her guard and tell him what he wanted to know about Brance Fortier. He'd been all over town this morning, and nobody even admitted seeing the outlaw leave. Fortier'd probably threatened them.

Two identical platters of food banged down between them. "Would there be anything else, sir?"

Clayton kept his eyes locked with Irene's. "Yeah. Add a canteen of coffee to those sandwiches, will you?"

"Certainly, sir."

He reached his good arm across the table and covered Irene's small, manicured hand. "Well?"

The starch drained out of her. He'd set it up just right, he thought in satisfaction. She'd taken the bait. She'd be bored and talkative within an hour, and he was an expert at ferreting out information.

She looked him in the eye. "May I have your word of honor you will not attempt to compromise me, Mr. Black?"

"My word of honor." No risk there, he thought. She was his link to Fortier; he'd treat her with velvet gloves. His gut told him the outlaw was long gone, and he ached to be after him. But he figured he could spare three more hours, tops, if it would save him some time later on. Otherwise, he'd have to try to pick up a cold trail, and that was slow and tedious. This way, he could save a day, maybe two.

Besides, he liked the company of this prickly lady lawyer with an unexpected aptitude for five-card draw. At the moment, gazing into her up-turned face, watching her rosy lips open to admit a dainty forkful of ham, he didn't know which he wanted more—breakfast or Irene Hardisson.

Watch it, mi amigo. *In your line of work, a woman like this is a dead end.*

He knew that, all right. Had known it for years.

Being a Ranger's wife is no kinda life for a woman, his father had said. *Every single day, she's just one rifle bullet away from widowhood.*

Part of him acknowledged the raw truth of the words. Another part of him was so desperately alone he didn't care about the risk.

Forget it, you dumb son of a gun. You know what you have to do. And you know the price.

God's little scorpions, sometimes he wished that sensible part of him would just shut the hell up.

"It's a package," Irene said at last.

Clayton started. "A deal," he corrected. Suddenly he wished he'd never proposed the idea. The thought of Irene and himself out in a grassy meadow somewhere made him feel hot all over. He'd sure like to do something other than watch a chess match.

He had to chuckle at that. Truth was, in spite of what Pa always said, he'd got this particular green-eyed woman kinda stuck in his throat.

Chapter Five

On the short buggy ride to Parker's Meadow—straight out of town on the Portland road the liveryman had instructed, then sharp right at the double oak trees—Clayton watched Irene fidget on the black leather seat beside him. Plain as buttered pancakes she was itching to do *something,* but he'd lay odds it wasn't rolling along in a buggy so close to him her skirt brushed his thigh.

The instant they crested the rise and the meadow spread before them like a rich green carpet, she settled down. Far across the swath of long grass two men dressed in black sat motionless at a makeshift table, its legs hidden in the lush grass.

The chess players. Clayton shot a glance at Irene and frowned. Her gaze was riveted on the two figures hunched over the table. Her eyes sparkled. "Can you go any faster?"

Faster? He didn't expect her to be *this* interested.

Then again, she wasn't like most women he'd known.

Which, he acknowledged, had been few and far between. He let out a long breath. All his life he'd taken pains to mask his Cherokee blood with white man's trappings, as his father had. The only concession he made to his Indian heritage was refusing to cut his hair but once each year. Out here in untamed Oregon, he didn't look too different from anybody else, but he wondered what Irene would say if she knew about his Cherokee side, how he'd been shunned in both worlds, Indian and white. How uncomfortable he felt in towns like this, or with a woman like her.

As they drew near, Irene leaned forward, her hands clasped in her lap. Clayton pulled the rig into an area of flattened grass and set the brake. A few saddle horses raised their heads, then returned to their desultory cropping of the grass at their feet.

It was a perfect afternoon, Clayton noted. He considered unhitching the mare, then thought better of it. Irene would be bored and hungry in an hour—two at the most. When she grew tired of watching the game she'd want to head back to town—or, better still, lounge on the meadow and have a picnic with him. And then she'd start talking about Fortier.

He could hardly wait. He turned to speak to her, but she was gone. "Now where the hell…"

A flash of blue sateen drew his eyes to the small table set under a spreading oak. Two motionless players in long black frock coats and soft black caps atop their gray heads sat like two large blackbirds, bent over the chessboard between them. Irene positioned herself to one side, folded her arms across her waist and watched.

Clayton waited for her to move or shift position, but she remained still as a blue-clad statue. Purposefully he circled the small gathering of onlookers, watching Irene, who in turn studied the chess pieces with as much intensity as the two rail-thin players. Russians, someone at the hotel had said. Homesteading adjacent plots of land in Crazy Creek Valley, the two met every Friday to play chess.

Irene watched the game with unwavering intensity, moving only once to shoo away a bumblebee. The sun climbed high overhead, slipped off center and began to descend.

Clayton began to pace. He hadn't anticipated her complete absorption in the proceedings; her look of rapt fascination made him just a tad uneasy. He craved some talk about events concerning Brance Fortier's disappearance, but at the moment she was plainly interested only in the chess match.

He walked about the meadow in ever-widening circles, skirting the fringe of fir trees where afternoon shadows began to lengthen, frustration building inside him. On his next loop near the chess table, he studied Irene for signs of flagging interest. She never even looked up at him.

With a groan, Clayton tramped back to the buggy, loosened the harness and removed the bit from the horse's mouth. No sense keeping the rig at the ready—Irene was lost in the game.

Another hour crept by and she didn't move an inch. Maybe he'd better give up on the idea of a quiet interrogation under the guise of polite picnic conversation.

Or maybe he had a better idea. Noiselessly he edged close to Irene, leaned forward and breathed a single word into her ear. "Lunch?"

"Oh, yes," she whispered without moving. Her gaze pinned on the game before her, she stuck out her hand. "A sandwich, if you please."

Clayton plopped a small towel-wrapped bundle into her outstretched palm and watched her unwrap it. She nibbled at the slice of chicken poking out between the slices of bread. While he watched her take occasional dainty bites, her attention glued to the chessboard, he devoured four sandwiches and washed them down with a swig of lukewarm coffee from a glass jar. He wished like anything it was whiskey. This whole charade was getting his dander up.

Irene Hardisson had said barely three words in as many hours. Only a scattering of pieces re-

mained on the board, but neither of the solemn-
face men had made a move in the past thirty
minutes. The game was at a standstill.

No one moved. No one spoke. Irene swallowed
the last of her sandwich and stood as if transfixed,
her eyes on the board. She cradled her chin in her
palm, frowning.

About time, Clayton thought with a rush of hope.
She's gettin' bored. He'd just sidle around to her
side and ease her away for a private chat.

He touched her elbow, cupped his fingers about
the rounded bone and gave a gentle tug.

Irene stood solid as a brick chimney. He pulled
again. "Irene," he whispered. "It's about time
we—"

"Hush!" she hissed.

Clayton released her arm and glanced skyward.
Lord help him! He'd been outmaneuvered by a
stubborn lady and two old Russian farmers. When
he lowered his gaze, he noted the sun just touched
the tips of the tall firs encircling the meadow. Another hour and they wouldn't be able to see the
chessboard!

Clayton gritted his teeth. His shoulder was beginning to ache. His feet, too. Most of the tracking
he did was on horseback; he wasn't used to a lot
of walking.

But Irene's interest showed no sign of flagging.
In fact, she didn't look the least bit tired. Or bored.

Her face was lit up like a child's at a candy counter.

Clayton jammed his good hand into his trouser pocket and rocked back on his heels. No, she was definitely not bored. And definitely not chattering to him about Brance Fortier, as he had planned. Devil take the girl!

Give it up, amigo. *You made a bad bargain.*

He hated to think about the time he'd wasted out here. What was worse, he grumbled to himself as he strode another circuit around the meadow, she hadn't done it intentionally. Hell and damn. He'd best go feed an apple to that patient mare he'd tied up beside the buggy.

Just as he started to leave, a small sound broke the silence. A carved wooden chess piece, a king, Clayton recognized, lay tipped on its side in the center of the board.

"All right, Isaac," one of the men muttered. "You vin."

"Mmm-hmm, Mordecai, vat I tell you?"

"Wait!" a feminine voice ordered. "Queen to bishop three!"

Clayton froze. Both men's eyes turned toward Irene.

"I mean," Irene stammered, "if you move your queen to…"

One of the black-clad men leaped to his feet. "Isaac, look! Iss the Hostage Lady!"

Aghast, Irene stared at the man. The Hostage Lady? Was that what she was called? Good gracious!

She sneaked a glance at the lean, tanned Texas Ranger who stood off to one side, one hand in his pocket, eyeing her with sudden interest. Mercy! She most certainly did not relish the thought of Mr. Black's finding out her role in that hostage matter. Clayton Black had been trailing that man—Brance Fortier—the very man she had helped to escape. If it weren't for her, the outlaw would still be languishing in the Crazy Creek jail.

The taller of the two chess players leaped to his feet, snatched the cap off his head and bowed low. "Most honored, Missus Lady. You safe my son, Benjamin. Trade him for that horse thief! Be seated, please!"

The other man, Isaac, whipped a bandanna from his vest pocket and ceremoniously dusted off the crude chair his friend had vacated. "Please, sit, lady. Please!" He clasped one arm over his middle and bowed from the waist.

"Oh, please, I—" Irene gripped the back of the hand-hewn chair. "I only meant to say you need not concede—there is one move you can make to checkmate, you see?" She pointed to the chessboard. "With your opponent's king exposed as it is, all you have to do is advance your queen—"

"*Nyet!* Game iss not important, now." Mordecai, at least she thought that was his name, waved one long arm over the table. "*You* are important! You are Hostage Lady, who talk to outlaw and get my son back for me."

"Oh, no, I merely…" Irene shrank inwardly at the sudden expression of anger that crossed Clayton Black's regular features. One black eyebrow twitched upward. He yanked his hand out of his pocket and held it up.

"Well, now," he drawled, "I don't believe I've heard this part of the story."

Isaac beamed. "Oh, she was so brave! So smart!"

"Smart," Clayton repeated in a quiet voice. His eyes burned into hers with such intensity she could not look away. Her cheeks grew hot. She didn't want the lawman to hear this, didn't want to acknowledge her part in freeing the murderer he had chased all the way from Texas.

"And brave, too!" Isaac reminded with enthusiasm. His Adam's apple bobbed up and down.

"Brave, too, huh?" Clayton nodded, holding her gaze. "It figures."

Mordecai's bony hands tugged at the top button on his coat. "All day she talk to sheriff, then to outlaw, then again to sheriff. Then it gets late, and she walks alone down the street and outlaw, he walks from opposite with his hand on my son's neck, and they meet in middle, in front of saloon."

"And that's how Fortier got away," Clayton supplied. The edge in his voice sent a shiver up Irene's spine.

"Miss Hardisson, you played right into Fortier's hands."

"But I had to do it, Mr. Black. He threatened to shoot the boy!"

Mordecai wrung his hands together. "She safe my Benjamin's life, iss vat she does!"

"Eye for eye, life for life!" Isaac added.

"Yeah," Clayton said softly.

Something flickered in the unsettling gray eyes. As she watched, an odd glitter in their depths hardened to stone.

Irene stiffened her spine. She was sorry Fortier had slipped through his fingers, but she most certainly was *not* sorry that Mordecai's son was alive and well.

"Missus Law Lady?" Mordecai stepped forward and grasped both her hands. With a sigh of gratitude, he raised her knuckles to his lips. "My wife and I, ve are grateful."

Clayton Black spun on his heel and the next thing she knew he was striding away from her toward the buggy, his long black hair swinging in rhythm with his steps.

She bid a hasty goodbye to the chess players and caught up with him just as he slipped the bit into the horse's mouth.

"Mr. Black, I—well, I am sorry."

"What for?" He kept his back to her. "With lawyers like you around, killers'd go free every day of the week."

The remark stung. "Now just one minute, Mr. High-and-Mighty. What, if I may be so inquisitive, would *you* have done under the circumstances?"

"First off, I'd have kept Fortier locked up."

"He was released on bail—a perfectly legal undertaking. How was I to know he'd steal a gun and—"

"Second thing, I'd have shot him the minute he laid a hand on the boy."

Irene gasped. "But what if you missed? What if you hit poor young Benjamin instead?"

With his good arm, Clayton dropped the harness over the mare's head. "I wouldn't have missed. And I sure as hell wouldn't have let him walk away scot-free. Hellfire, woman, there's a price on his head!"

Irene straightened her spine. "First of all, at the time I was unaware of that fact. Mr. Fortier may have been wanted in Texas, but he was arrested in Oregon for horse theft. May I remind you, Mr. Black, that under the provisions of the constitution, an accused man is considered innocent until proven guilty by a jury of his peers."

"Bullfeathers. Everyone knows horse thieves get hanged."

"Horse thieves are entitled to their day in court, like everyone else!" Irene's voice shook with indignation. "Even murderers are presumed innocent until—"

"Shut up, Miss Hardisson. Just shut the hell up." He left the horse and strode toward her. Without so much as a "by your leave" he closed his arm about her waist, lifted her off the ground and deposited her in the buggy. "It'll be a cold day in hell when I want a lecture on the rights of scum like Brance Fortier. I'll drive you home."

He climbed in beside her, flapped the reins and the buggy lurched forward.

Irene sat down hard on the seat, clamped her teeth together until her jaw ached, and fought back angry tears. How could he be so pigheaded? So close-minded? And he called himself a lawman. Why, the very idea! Didn't they have schools in Texas? Didn't they teach about the U.S. Constitution?

All the way back to town she seethed in silence. When they turned onto Main Street, Clayton's spoken words nearly jolted her out of her skin.

"So, you already knew how to play chess." It was an observation, not a question.

Startled, Irene shot him a look and nodded. "My father taught me. I have never witnessed a match, however."

"You know, Miss Hardisson, I wasted a whole

day out here, waiting for you to get bored so we could talk.''

All of a sudden her every sense came alive. ''Talk? Talk about what?''

''About Brance Fortier. You gonna tell me which way he was headed last time you saw him?''

Irene sighed. Absurd disappointment washed through her. He wanted to talk…business. Always business. All he wanted was Fortier, and for some reason that nettled her. ''Yesterday I didn't want to tell you. I still don't.''

''You don't,'' Clayton echoed.

''But…well, I do feel somewhat responsible for complicating your job, Mr. Black.''

''And?'' His voice sounded as if it were muffled in velvet.

Irene swallowed. The softer his tone, the more uneasy she grew. Clayton Black exuded a mesmerizing power. It wasn't just the look of the man, tall and rangy with that smooth, easy way he had of moving. There was something else about him, something that frightened her and that drew her, as well. He was…different. She sensed a barely contained wildness just beneath the surface.

''Mr. Fortier headed out of town on the Portland road. But I don't think he continued west. I climbed Schoolhouse Hill to watch, and I think he may have circled around and headed north.''

Clayton grunted. ''Why didn't you tell me this

at breakfast? I could have saved a basket of sandwiches and a whole day rambling around that
meadow on foot, waiting for you to fold up.''

Irene gave him a long, direct look, opened her
mouth to speak and then closed it. ''I—I really
wanted to go on the picnic.''

''And why was that, Miss Hardisson?''

She hesitated. ''Because,'' she managed, feeling
her cheeks warm. ''Because…well, I have always
wanted to…to see a chess match.''

She closed her eyes to avoid the sudden heat in
his gaze.

Clayton guided the buggy back into town, torn
between anger and admiration for Irene's gambit.
Part of him wanted to throttle the young woman
who perched next to him, the toes of her shoes held
primly together on the buggy floor. Another part
of him wanted to laugh out loud.

He'd laid his trap with such care, and then he'd
walked right into it. What kind of damn fool did
that make him?

He bit back a groan. One who liked looking at
Irene Hardisson's small hands, folded in her lap,
her rose-tinged cheeks and the pale, smooth skin
of her exposed neck when she bent her head—even
that ridiculous hat with the cherries on top. His
eyes devoured her as his brain grappled with his
next move.

They swung onto Main Street, and Clayton breathed in the warm, rose-scented air and tried to sort out his options. So Fortier had started toward Portland, then turned north. A lucky break. He'd be easier to track in open country, especially on foot. It'd take the outlaw some time to steal a horse—*another* horse—and then he'd be halfway to Canada.

Now that he thought it over, maybe Irene had helped him more than she knew. If he could get word to the Mounties, they could stop Fortier at the border. That made his job simple, but it didn't exactly make him happy. He wanted to make the capture himself. In fact, he itched to start right now—the minute he deposited the Hostage Lady safely on her front porch.

That thought sobered him. Yeah, ride out tonight and leave her behind. Why not? He could cover a lot of ground before dark—enough to get him out of civilization and pick up Fortier's trail.

He flapped the reins, and the mare broke into a trot. He'd never have to deal with Crazy Creek again. Or Irene, either.

Hell and blazes. He brought the horse to a standstill. He didn't mind leaving Crazy Creek—one white steeple town in a lifetime was plenty for him. But Irene?

You have a job to do, amigo! *And it doesn't leave room for lady-courting.*

Right. He had to get on with it.

At that moment, Irene turned toward him and laid a hesitant hand on his arm. "You drove right past my house, Mr. Black. It's the big white one, with the wraparound porch, remember?"

Clayton grunted. He trotted the horse past the hotel and the Silver Swan Saloon, swung a wide turn in the road at the edge of town and headed back in the opposite direction.

"You got a telegraph office in this town?"

"Not here. But I believe there is one in Cedarville. Why?"

"Thought I'd warn the Canadian authorities that Fortier's headed their way."

"Oh, there's no need for that. Sheriff Calder is sure to capture him."

"Thought you said the sheriff was off hunting?"

"That is correct. Sheriff Calder is hunting Brance Fortier. He has a posse with him."

"Posse!"

"That is what I said. Mr. Oberst, the tailor, and two or three ranchers, and let's see, who else? Oh, yes, the bartender at the Silver Swan. Curly, I think his name is. They all took guns."

"Amateurs," Clayton grumbled. "God help them. They'll never even catch sight of a fish as slippery as Fortier. Be lucky if they don't accidentally shoot each other!"

"Oh, I don't think so," Irene retorted. "I see the sheriff now, coming toward us."

Clayton's head jerked up. Sure enough, five or six horses barreled down the street, raising a cloud of dust you could barely see through.

Clayton frowned. Hold on a minute. Something was wrong.

Chapter Six

"Mercy!" Irene cried. The sight of Sheriff Calder at the other end of the street, slumped over the pommel of his saddle, made her gasp. "Whatever can be the matter with him?"

"I'd wager he's been shot." Clayton snapped the reins and the buggy hurtled to where the sheriff's exhausted horse had plodded to a halt. The injured man tipped sideways, one hand clasped over his middle.

"Here!" Clayton handed the reins to Irene and vaulted out of the buggy. She calmed the nervous mare and watched Clayton take the sheriff's considerable bulk onto his good shoulder and lever him off the horse. He straightened under the burly man's weight and gently walked him to the boardwalk. "Hurt bad?"

"Gut shot," the sheriff grunted. "One of my posse got the jitters and his revolver discharged."

"Lucky you weren't killed," Clayton said quietly. "Where's the posse now?"

"Still out chasin' Fortier."

Clayton gave a short, hard laugh. "A tailor, a bartender, and three ranchers? They haven't got an angel's chance in hell. C'mon. Got to get you to a doctor."

"Just down the street," Irene volunteered. "On the left. Put him in the buggy."

"No." Clayton bent his knees and pivoted so his chest butted against the sheriff's meaty shoulder. Then he straightened and lifted the man off his feet.

"Go tell the doc we're comin'," he ordered.

Irene scrambled out of the buggy and flew down the street. Behind her she heard labored breathing—whether the sheriff's or Clayton Black's she could not tell. By the time Dr. Tyler's office door swung open, she could almost distinguish between the Ranger's grunts and the sheriff's wheezy groans.

Clayton carefully dumped the sheriff onto a sheet-swathed examining table.

Sweat stood out on Sheriff Calder's paste-colored face. "Mister?"

"Shut your mouth, Jim," the doctor snapped. "'Less you want to bleed to death before I get your belly sewed up." He lifted the torn shirt and bright blood welled out of a ragged wound the size of her fist. Unexpectedly her knees felt wobbly. She'd seen blood before, but not like this! She grabbed at Clayton's arm to steady herself.

"Get her outta here," Dr. Tyler snapped.

"I am perfectly all right," she protested.

Clayton slipped his good arm around Irene's waist. "Let's go, Miss Hardisson."

"Wait!" the sheriff wheezed.

"Can't. Lady's about to faint, and Fortier's still on the loose." He walked her toward the door.

"Mister...don't go after him."

"Shut up, Jim." Dr. Tyler's stern voice was punctuated by the clank of metal instruments in an enamelware pan.

"Posse's useless, mister. Somebody else'll get shot. Listen, will ya? Fortier's on foot. Can't get far."

Irene felt Clayton hesitate. "Yeah?"

"I can deputize you. Town needs a sheriff. Wait till I can walk—two days, maybe three. When the posse gives up and comes in, you can pick up his trail and catch up easy."

Irene spun toward the wheezing man on the examining table. "Oh, that won't be necessary, Sheriff. Mr. Black is himself a lawman. A Texas Ranger."

The doctor's bushy gray eyebrows waggled upward. "That so?"

"Please…" the sheriff gasped "I got a feelin'. Stay…watch over Crazy Creek. I got a feelin'…."

"My job's to bring in Fortier, not nursemaid a— a town like this." Clayton clamped his jaw shut. *A white steeple town,* he'd almost said. That's the last thing he needed, keeping law and order in the kind of place he knew would turn on him the minute they learned he was half Cherokee.

Watch over this town? No way on God's green earth.

Irene tipped her face up to his. "We do need a peace officer here," she murmured. "And, if you stay, perhaps I could teach you to play chess?"

"Already know how," Clayton said shortly.

"Well, then—poker. We could play some additional rounds of poker, could we not?"

"Hands," he corrected automatically.

"Sheriff's right," Dr. Tyler chimed in. "Gotta have protection for the townsfolk. What if that outlaw fellow circles around and comes back?"

"Please, Mr.…Black, is it? A Texas Ranger…just what we…" The sheriff's voice began to fade as the physician waved a wad of liquid-soaked cotton under his nose.

Clayton turned away from the sickly sweet odor of ether. Yanking open the door, he breathed in gulps of the fresh evening air. Behind him he heard the zing of ripping fabric and the doctor's low grunt.

"Not too deep," the physician muttered. He sent Clayton a meaningful look. "Be up and about in a couple of days. How 'bout it?"

The question hung in the warm, still air as the doctor continued to work. He opened his mouth to refuse the offer when Irene's green eyes locked with his.

"Truth poker," she murmured. "Such a challenging game. Don't you find it so, Mr. Black?"

In his mind's eye he saw Irene seated across from him, her soft eyes looking into his, her lips parting to speak. Then he saw Brance Fortier picking his way across the mountains on foot. The man couldn't cover more than ten or fifteen miles a day; on horseback, Clay could overtake him in a single day.

Besides, it'd be suicide to ride out after a green, trigger-happy posse that didn't know him from Adam. He'd already been shot in the shoulder— once around that barn was enough.

He guessed he could take on the sheriff's role for now and ride out later, when the posse straggled in. Three days of easy duty would give his shoulder time to heal up, maybe even let him get in a little practice with his shooting arm.

And just thinking about three long nights playing poker with the prettiest lawyer west of the Mississippi made his skin tingle. There were some things about her he'd give his eyeteeth to know—

like what she thought about at night. What she
wanted in life. What she looked like underneath all
those flounces.

What she'd taste like.

That settled it. He'd stay. For a while. A *short*
while. Might do him good to hang his hat somewhere he was actually wanted for a change.

But he'd have to tread real careful when it came
to Miss Irene. She was not a rambling rose, not
one bit. She was all civilized and ladified—all fluff
and feathers, Pa would have said. She would expect things nice and proper.

He heaved an unconscious sigh and ushered her
outside onto the wood sidewalk. No sense gettin'
his blood up or her hopes raised; he wasn't ever
going to be the settling-down type.

Listening to himself, he almost laughed out loud.
He'd let himself get talked into staying and already
he was issuing "nice and proper" orders to his
hungry male body. But by jingo, he was a man,
not a statue!

He could play the part of sheriff for a few days.
But how long could he play the part of a gentleman
around soft, sweet-smelling Irene Hardisson?

Long enough, he told himself. He wouldn't compromise her. And he'd work damn hard to keep
her from sticking in his memory when he rode on
his way.

*   *   *

A worse beginning as acting sheriff of Crazy Creek Clayton couldn't imagine. After depositing Irene safely on her front porch he'd stopped in at the Silver Swan. Big mistake.

With the bartender away ridin' posse, he was informed, drinks were served up by shifts of volunteers. Tonight's civic-minded helper turned out to be the town drunk, Lysander Pettigrew. Lysander was so bleary-eyed by the time Clayton got there he was pouring out shots of hair tonic instead of whiskey.

Clayton arrested him so he wouldn't poison any of the customers. He marched the weaving man out the saloon door and down the street to the jail behind the sheriff's office and spent the rest of the night listening to the same off-key version of "She'll Be Comin' Round the Mountain" until his head ached.

When the sun finally rose, Pettigrew curled up on his jail cell cot to sleep it off and Clayton closed his eyes with a groan of relief. God Almighty, he was tired. Sitting behind a desk guarding a prisoner all night was worse than tracking an outlaw across unknown territory during a rainstorm.

He sure felt like a fish out of water in this town. No cantina with pretty women to dance with, no all-night card games. Just the snoring of Lysander Pettigrew in the back cell and a sore butt from the sheriff's hard wooden desk chair. He dozed off thinking of Texas tea cakes, the leathery pancakes he and his father often fried up on the trail.

He woke when a determined feminine voice inquired, "Are you off duty or on?"

"Off," he muttered from under his hat.

"Wake up, Mr. Black. I'm here on business."

Clayton cracked one eyelid. At the sight of shiny red cherries drooping over a straw hat brim, he forced his stiff body into an upright position.

"Mr. Black," Irene announced.

Each syllable of his name was crisply enunciated. Something in her tone made him sit up straighter. "Miss Hardisson?"

"I understand you arrested Lysander Pettigrew last night." She regarded him with cool green eyes, her mouth unsmiling.

"I did that, yes." He couldn't wrench his gaze from her lips. When her pink tongue slipped out to wet her lips, his groin tightened.

Clayton fought to keep his train of thought. "Mr. Pettigrew got himself so sozzled at the Silver Swan he was a danger to himself and the customers."

The pink tongue disappeared. "Mr. Pettigrew," she replied, "is a sweet, harmless man who wouldn't hurt a fly."

Frustration and the ache in his groin brought him to his feet. "Miss Hardisson, you're full of…cotton balls!"

She stiffened her spine and advanced a step toward him. "You are to release your prisoner this instant!"

Clayton inhaled her delicate lilac-and-spice scent and closed his hands into fists. "I am, huh?"

"That is correct, you are."

"Now hold on a minute, ma'am. I'm the law here until Sheriff Calder recovers. Pettigrew's inside sleeping it off and I'm not about to let him out until tonight when the Silver Swan closes. He's too dangerous."

"You are mistaken in your assumption, Mr. Black. You are not 'the law' here—you merely uphold the law as the courts interpret it. Under the provisions of the constitution," she added with a little sniff. She licked her lips again.

Clayton gritted his teeth. "Scuttlebutt I picked up last night says Pettigrew's the town drunk. He's dangerous, like I said. Hair tonic can be lethal."

"That is immaterial," she snapped. "I insist you release the man. I will expect him to walk out of here a free man within the hour."

Something about her combative stance—hands on her hips, shoulders straight, eyes flashing—combined with the soft-looking green dress edged with ruffles and ivory lace struck him as so incongruous he stared at her, openmouthed, for a full minute.

"And if I don't?"

"If you do not, I will get a court order from Judge Phipps over in Cedarville."

He had her now. "Forget it. By the time you ride over to Cedarville and back, Pettigrew will be cold sober and the Silver Swan will be locked up tight. I'll release him then in any case."

"Now," she persisted. "You will release him now. You cannot hold a man simply because he *might* commit a crime." The lace encircling her neckline trembled with indignation.

She had him there, he acknowledged. Thank the Lord she was in Oregon and not Texas. Every Ranger within a hundred miles of her would spit bullets or die laughing over her constitution-and-the-law speech. She might have a point all right, but no self-respecting lawman ever followed those rules to bring an outlaw to justice. Took too damn long.

She folded her arms across her waist. The toe of one black leather shoe began to tap the floor. "Mr. Black?" she reminded.

Clayton jumped as if he'd been shot. He'd been woolgathering, watching that fluttering lace and imagining the warm, silken flesh that lay beneath it.

He wrenched his mind back to the problem at hand. "All right, give me a minute."

"Very well. One minute."

He pivoted, tramped past the potbellied stove

into the back room where his prisoner sprawled on a jail cell cot. "Wake up. There's a lawyer to see you."

When he returned with an unsteady Lysander Pettigrew in tow, Irene nodded her approval. The cherries on her hat bobbed up and down.

"I knew you would see it my way," she caroled. "Mr. Black, your intelligence is admirable. Thank you, and good morning!"

She disappeared through the doorway in a whisper of petticoats, Mr. Pettigrew trailing in her wake.

Clayton settled for a citified breakfast of flapjacks at the Maybud Hotel and thought about how to tame Miss Law-and-Order. He mulled the prospect over for the remainder of the sun-scorched July day, and when the opportunity presented itself later that afternoon, he was ready.

"Hold on, Miss Hardisson, you wanna run that by me again?"

Irene signed in exasperation. "My client, Elias Simms, arrived from New York just yesterday morning and purchased two horses for twenty-five dollars apiece from Mr. Thorncroft at the livery stable."

"So?"

"So when he went to pick them up, Mr. Black,

there was only one horse! Mr. Simms has been cheated.''

Clayton swung his feet off the sheriff's desk and stood up. ''Not cheated, just boondoggled.''

''Boondoggled! Is that some kind of Texas term for thievery?''

''Miss Hardisson, I can see it falls to me to teach you a thing or two about customs out west. A greenhorn fresh from New York is fair game, you *sabe?*''

''I do not,'' she huffed. ''I recognize a swindle when I see one. Either my client gets his twenty-five dollars back or he deserves another horse from Mr. Thorncroft. Or—'' she twitched her skirts in disgust ''—Mr. Thorncroft can spend some time in jail.''

His eyes narrowed. ''Is that so?''

''Yes.''

''You know, when you get all fluffed up over something, you look just like the little banty chicken my momma used to have.''

In spite of herself, Irene gasped. A chicken? He compared her to a chicken? She stood before him, demanding justice, and the sheriff—the *acting* sheriff, she reminded herself—called her a chicken?

''That is immaterial,'' she snapped. ''The law is the law. My client demands satisfaction.''

''Your client's been bested in the oldest game

on the frontier—makin' a jackass out of a green-horn. Down South, we call it the Texas Two-Step. Fella comes in, wants to buy a horse. So we run one out for him—all saddled and everything, and he looks it over. 'Got anything else?' he's sure to ask, since he doesn't know beans about horseflesh. The farmer says 'Sure do,' and takes the horse back into the barn, waits a few minutes, and then brings out the same horse with a different saddle—maybe an English style—and a different colored saddle blanket. 'You can have 'em both for fifty dollars.' Easterners fall for it every time.''

"But that's cheating!"

"It's a hoodwinker, all right, but it's harmless enough. The greenhorn loses twenty-five dollars, and everybody gets a good laugh. If he takes it good, it counts for him later on.''

Irene moved to stand toe-to-toe with the Ranger. "You—" she jabbed a forefinger at his chest "—are a menace to law-abiding citizens every-where. Why, I never heard such nonsense."

"People don't laugh much in Philadelphia, I reckon."

"Really, Mr. Black. No one laughs at dishon-esty, east or west.''

"Wanna bet?" His gray eyes regarded her with a challenge in their depths.

"Bet? Whatever do you mean?"

"I'll bet you Sheriff Calder will laugh out loud when you tell him Mr. Simms's horse problem."

"He most certainly will not! He will order you to arrest Mr. Thorncroft immediately, and I shall have the laugh."

"Wanna bet on that, too?"

He held her gaze until she felt her midsection begin to dissolve. She couldn't imagine why that man's eyes did funny things to her stomach.

"I certainly would!" She snapped out the words without thinking. She could never resist any kind of gamble. Besides, she relished the chance to make him eat his words.

"Done," he quipped. He offered his good hand.

Anxious to be off to visit the sheriff, Irene clasped it for a brief moment but found she couldn't withdraw it. He held her fingers tight in his grip, drew her toward him and spoke.

"If you win, I'll pledge two hours of my time for any task you name."

Irene tugged her hand away, smiling in satisfaction at the thought of putting the tall lawman to work sloshing paste on the three rolls of flowered wallpaper waiting in her dining room. "Agreed."

"And if you lose…" He let the sentence trail off as a calculating look came into his eyes. "If you lose," he continued, his voice low and husky, "you owe me two hours of *your* time."

Her heart caught. "Doing what?"

"Anything I say. Within the bounds of propriety, of course," he added.

She was tempted. She couldn't wait to see his face when she showed him the wallpaper! How pleased Nora would be when she arrived next week to find the walls covered and the draperies Mrs. Webster was sewing already pressed and hung up on rods.

Without another word, she whirled away and flew out the door and down the street to the doctor's office.

The sheriff's face turned scarlet against the white bedsheet. "Haw, haw, haw! Ouch, it shore hurts to laugh, little lady. But that's a good one, all right—bought the same horse twice, did he? Haw, haw!"

Behind her Irene heard Clayton Black give a discreet cough. "Two whole hours," he murmured just loud enough for her to hear.

Taken aback by the sheriff's unexpected response, Irene acknowledged with growing consternation that she'd lost the bet. At the moment, it didn't bear thinking about. She had to make a graceful exit, find Mr. Simms and advise him he'd been the butt of a joke rather than the victim of chicanery. After that…

Well, after that Clayton Black could just come looking for her if he wanted to claim his winnings.

Her brain whirled as a vision of rose wallpaper beckoned.

Maybe…just maybe, there might be a way to turn the tables on him.

Clayton finished up his rounds early. Lysander Pettigrew, sober as a Methodist, was tending bar at the Silver Swan. The schoolhouse bell had been restored after five gangly boys had wrestled it down from its perch and hidden it in the outhouse. Gray-bunned Olla Ames, the schoolmarm, set her students doing extra sums for the prank and sent a quavery smile to Clayton as thanks.

He'd checked in on Jim Calder, heard the doctor say the sheriff would be up and about in another day or so. Now, in the hot, windless afternoon, he found his footsteps drawn to the big white house across from the park.

Crazy Creek was a peaceful town, he thought as he tramped down Main Street. Not like any place he'd known in East Texas. The abnormal quiet of the place made his neck itch.

He didn't belong here. He felt it deep down inside his Cherokee bones. A town like this caught a man, bundled him up in a cocoon so tight he began to forget who he was or why he'd come. He was a Texas Ranger, he reminded himself. And half Indian.

Crazy Creek wouldn't catch him, Clayton

vowed. Not with Brance Fortier still on the loose
and Pa and Jannie to avenge. He didn't plan to stay
in Crazy Creek—hadn't planned to stay even this
long, but a certain green-eyed lady who smelled
like morning sunshine kept pulling him off balance.

Not exactly pulling, he amended as he crossed
the street. More like kicking him square in the
heart until he couldn't get her out of his mind. She
was soft and female and smart as blazes. Half the
time she scared the vinegar out of him; the other
half he ached for the feel of her body against his.

No matter. When the sheriff got himself out of
bed tomorrow, Clayton planned to leave. Tonight
would be the last time he'd see Irene Hardisson.

The thought made him feel a bit reckless. He
wouldn't compromise a lady, but he'd sure like to
taste that soft pink mouth just once before he rode
out.

"Why, Mr. Black. Good afternoon." She stood
on the white painted porch, looking at him through
the open front door.

Clayton tipped his hat. "Miss Hardisson."

"You've come to collect your bet, I presume?"
She didn't seem the least hesitant.

"Two hours of your time," Clayton reminded.

"Of course. Come in, won't you? I'm just fin-
ishing up my project for today."

Clayton stepped through the doorway, removed

his dust-stained gray hat, and almost tripped over a long-handled broom standing in a washtub of water. Long strips of paper lay on the bare floor, giant stripes against the dark wood.

"I'm wallpapering," she announced.

Clayton nodded. He wrinkled his nose at the floury smell of paste.

"If you could just hold down this end here, it will go much faster." She swished the broom in the water, then jammed the head into a wide-mouthed paste pot.

"What did you have in mind for your bet?" With quick, sure strokes, she brushed paste over one length of paper.

He started to open his mouth.

"Now, would you hold it up while I position it?" She guided him to the wall, pressed the sticky side of the paper to the plasterboard and smoothed it out with her hands. He watched her breasts lift when she raised her arms.

"I kinda had it in mind to take you to supper at the hotel and…"

She brushed paste onto another strip, pointing where she wanted it hung. "And?"

From behind the dripping panel, he heard the broom splash back into the washtub.

"Just a few more strips and I'll be finished. My, it does look nice, don't you think?"

Clayton stood, arm upheld, while Irene ducked

below his shoulder to smooth out the paper. The scent of her hair made his gut clench. Sweet and fresh, like sage blossoms after a rain.

"And," he continued when he found his voice, "then I thought I'd like to—"

"Lift that end, would you? Now, over here."

Hell's bells, she wasn't paying any mind to him! She hadn't heard one word he'd said. He suppressed a wry smile at his gullibility, then decided two could play at the game.

"...thought I'd like to put my arm around you and..."

"Over there, by the window. Higher. Now, a little to the left."

Clayton rolled his eyes toward the ceiling. "Hold you close to me," he finished in a low voice. Breath held, he waited for her response.

"More paste on this one, I think."

Jupiter! He was talking to the moon! "You listening, Miss Hardisson?"

"Right over here, please. Yes, of course I'm listening. Fold down that flap, would you?"

Clayton couldn't help chuckling. He folded, lifted, pasted as she directed, all the while murmuring under his breath what he'd like to do to her when the wallpapering was finished. "...touch you all over...taste you...kiss you three or four hundred times..." He grew hard just speaking the words.

"There, now—this is the last strip. Oh, that one's crook—four hundred times! Mr. Black, really!" Aghast, she faced him, the dripping broom in her hands.

Clayton laughed out loud. "You're getting paste-water all over your wood floor."

Her eyes widened. "What? Oh!" She sloshed the broom head along the length of the panel. "I do not wish to renege on a wager, Mr. Black, but a plan such as yours is quite out of the question."

Clayton lifted the final strip of dripping wallpaper and moved toward her. "You didn't hear half of what I said," he accused.

She sidestepped him. "Oh, but I did! Hang it right there, over the side door." She pointed.

"Miss Hardisson, you're lying through your teeth." He slapped the strip into place, pressed his palm down the length of the wall and suppressed a smile. "You thought you'd finagle me into this wallpapering business—" he gestured toward the washtub "—and I thought I'd soft-talk you into supper and a bit of spooning. For a fella who's won the wager, I think I got the short end of the stick, don't you?"

She didn't answer. He moved toward her, lifted the broom out of her grasp and tossed it aside. "The wallpapering's done. There's still time for supper. And," he added, "*after* supper."

She didn't move. Head up, she looked him in

the face but he could see the glimmer of apprehension in her eyes. He stepped nearer, touched her chin with his knuckles.

"I've wanted to kiss you since I first laid eyes on you."

The words floated out of him without conscious thought. Only when her breath hissed in did he realize he had spoken aloud.

She opened her mouth, wet her lips with a small, delicate tongue. "After supper?" she said in an unsteady voice. "I do not recall agreeing to 'after supper.' Besides, I have to rinse out the washtub and—and complete my day's agenda."

"No," he said quietly, "you don't. A deal's a deal, Miss Hardisson. Let's go."

Chapter Seven

The oddest things happened to her when she was near this man, Irene reflected. All the way down the street to the Maybud Hotel dining room, she had felt so light it was like floating, her black laced shoes barely skimming the board walkway. Her ears buzzed. Her brain seemed to grow moss.

"The lady will have steak and potatoes and gravy," Clayton announced to the grinning waitress. "I'll have the same."

She watched Clayton's lips move. Was he speaking to her or the serving girl? She lowered the menu.

"I'd like a steak, please. With roasted potatoes and lots of gravy."

A look passed between Clayton and the waitress.

"Yes, ma'am. Anything else?"

"Coffee," Clayton replied. "For two. Later."

Irene shook her head to clear the cobwebs. She

felt exactly as she had the day she'd fallen off her first pony.

"Coffee for me," she ordered. "After the meal, if you please."

A giggle escaped the girl's lips. Irene glanced at the lawman across the table from her.

Why does he look at me like that? The expression in his eyes mystified her. He looked...well, he looked like he wanted to devour her right here and now, and was trying to hide his smiling about the prospect. A delicious heat invaded her midsection. Her thoughts swirled inside her head like dry leaves.

My stars! She was an educated, disciplined attorney-at-law, reeling out of control at having dinner with this man, like a child's wooden hoop careening down a mountainside. What on earth ailed her?

Unease pricked a path up her spine, tickled the back of her neck. What *did* he have in mind for "after supper"? She gave a little shudder.

"Cold?" he inquired.

"No. Hot," she blurted without thinking. "I mean, the temperature of the room is quite adequate, thank you."

She sneaked a glance at him. The bones of his lean, tanned face, highlighted by the dining room chandelier, gave him a predatory look. His lips curved into a half smile, but the gray eyes remained expressionless. This was a man who worked to hide his feelings.

Which only whetted her curiosity. She preferred to understand things, especially complex things. And Clayton Black was complex.

Everything about him suggested an untamed wildness held under tight control, yet he looked and acted like everyone else—maybe more calm and sure of himself than most. His steady voice never rose, his manner was polite, his movements slow and purposeful. He never made an unnecessary motion.

So why was he fiddling with the salt cellar? She watched his long fingers twirl the china receptacle in place. She sensed a strength and purpose she had seen in few men. Despite the rough edges, he showed good breeding, though not of the Philadelphia sort. Hadn't he said his mother lived near New Orleans? A lady, probably.

Clayton was certainly no Southern gentleman, though. Neither did he seem like a back country rancher. He seemed an odd mix with his quiet manner and that chin-length black hair. He sported no mustache, but was clean shaven, his mouth exposed. Her heart gave a little jump.

She liked his mouth, studied the shape of his well-modeled lips. Without thinking, she fanned her face with her napkin. Clayton Black was more handsome, and more puzzling, than any man she'd ever met.

"Warm?" he inquired, his tone bland.

"Oh, no thank you. I'll have mine after supper."

Amusement lit his eyes for a second, then faded, and in its place flared a look of raw hunger. Then the curtain dropped again.

Her stomach somersaulted, and she looked away.

"Thirsty?" he murmured.

Oh, yes, she was parched! But not for anything as tangible as water. For…talk. For touch, even.

Her eyes burned with tears. She was lonely. For Papa, of course.

Fiddle-faddle, an inner voice stated. *Lonely, yes. But not for your papa.*

"For what, then?" she said aloud.

Clayton jerked at the sound of her voice, and the salt cellar wobbled.

For a man, said the voice. *This man.*

A plate of food plopped down in front of her. She grabbed her fork and stabbed the thick steak. Savory juices welled up between the tines.

"You might try a knife," Clayton remarked.

Irene stared at him. The squint lines around his eyes crinkled and she realized he was trying not to laugh.

"Well!" She stabbed again at her steak. *"Well!"* She couldn't unscramble her thoughts into a cohesive sentence, no matter how hard she tried.

Those unnerving eyes, and that lopsided smile of his...Lord have mercy, she was certainly not lonely for the likes of him!

She watched him reach into his vest and produce a narrow-bladed knife. With quick, expert motions he cut a slice off his steak, skewered it on the tip of the blade and brought it to his mouth. Fascinated, she watched him cut and eat two more bites. European style, she judged. Definitely not New Orleans.

"Thought you were hungry," he remarked.

Irene jerked at the sound of his voice. "What? Oh, no thank you—I'll use my own knife."

Again the softening, the amusement in his eyes. And then, just as quickly, they were shuttered. Desperate, she racked her brain for a gambit to turn the conversation.

"What other games do they play in Texas?"

Clayton looked up. "You've already lost one bet today—you sure you want to pursue this?"

Irene swallowed. She wanted to pursue something—anything—to get her thoughts off the way he moved his hands, the way he chewed his meat, slowly, as if savoring the taste, making the pleasure last as long as possible.

Her face burned. She cut a perfect small square of meat and closed her lips over it, swallowed it down. Her mouth was so dry it tasted like she'd taken a bite of yard goods.

"Too much wallpapering," Clayton said as if reading her thoughts. "The smell of paste kills some folks' appetite."

It wasn't the smell of wallpaper paste that made her insides jittery, she admitted. It was the nearness, the scent, of him—of soap and leather and sweat and…

She swirled another meat cube in the thick gravy and popped it into her mouth. Before she knew it, her plate was empty and a cup of hot coffee sat at her elbow.

Her breath caught. "After" dinner was getting closer.

Clayton leaned back in his chair and watched Irene run her fingertip around and around the inside of the cup handle. She was keyed up. Nervous. Maybe she *had* heard all his sweet talk this afternoon. Somehow he kept getting the impression she hadn't really been listening to him.

Maybe she'd be afraid to be alone with him now because of the things he'd said. His heart slammed against his ribs, and he had to laugh. *He* was the one who was scared! And this wasn't like him at all.

He liked Irene. Wanted her. And he knew about women—most of them were easy. But now…

Now he'd never been so terrified of a female.

Irene wasn't like *most* women. She wasn't like *any* woman. He grasped at a moment of unsettling clarity.

Well, compadre, *deep down inside you know what this means—time to say adios.*

His coffee grew cold. Hers disappeared and the waitress refilled her cup, which she sipped slowly in the silence. Clayton couldn't get his legs to move.

"We play a game called Texas One-up," he heard himself say. He was killing time. He knew it, but he couldn't help himself. He wanted to prolong being with her, make it last and last. He wanted to be with her, but he knew the minute he made a move, it'd be all over.

He drew a deck of cards from his vest pocket. "You cut the deck, see." He laid the cards on the table.

"Double or nothing?" he said softly.

Instantly she came to life. She sent him a calculating look. "If I win, I owe you nothing. If you win…" She faltered.

"You owe me double," he finished for her. "Four hours instead of two."

"Four hours! Why, half the night is already gone—it would be most unseemly to be alone and unchaperoned in the middle of the—"

"Listen, Irene. We're not talking about 'seemly.' We're talking about a debt of honor."

They stared at each other for a full minute. Then she reached out an unsteady hand and cut the deck.

A four of clubs lay faceup on the tablecloth. Without a word, Clayton made a second cut.

But he didn't look at the card. Instead, he rejoined the two halves of the deck, slid the cards into his pocket, and stood up.

"Come on. I just decided I don't want this to be on account of a card game. I want it to be just you and me."

She preceded him through the doorway and down the front steps of the hotel. He walked her along the deserted street in silence, his hand lightly cupping her elbow.

She snugged the blue wool shawl she wore around her shoulders and he tightened his fingers under her elbow. All the way to the park, neither one of them said a word.

Just as she started across the street toward her house, he stopped, turned her partway toward him and stepped in close. He wanted her so much he ached.

"Irene."

She lifted her head, and he caught her mouth under his.

Her mouth was like silk, smooth and so sweet his throat closed. He kept his hand on her waist, fighting the urge to move it over her back, touch her breasts.

She lifted her arms and encircled his neck. Dislodged from her shoulders, the shawl fell away, and Clayton caught it, then encircled her with his arm. Endless seconds stretched while he held her and the kiss lengthened, deepened.

He was lost. He knew it the instant his lips met hers.

And he had to let her go. Had to.

Irene clung to him and made a small sound. This was madness. Heaven. A dream. His mouth asked, and hers answered, as if some being deep inside her with a will of its own fought to be freed and then reveled in capture. In possession.

She opened to him with an abandon that shocked her. She could not think, could only feel. She wanted the taste of his mouth never to end.

When Clayton finally released her, he was so shaken he could not reason. The thought of not touching her again, never seeing that silly hat with the cherries on it, hearing her voice echo his restaurant orders when she was flustered, watching those green eyes snap when she was absorbed in a challenge—wallpaper, a chess match, a poker hand…

Oh, God. His chest felt like a fist pummeled it.

He reached for her again. Dimly he became aware of hoofbeats coming down the street, two—

maybe three horses. Coming fast. Instinctively he turned Irene so his body shielded hers.

"There he is!" a man shouted. "Get 'im, boys!"

Out of the corner of his eye, Clayton saw the flash of gunfire. No sound, just the flare of hot, white light.

The bullet went wide. Keeping Irene at his back, Clayton whirled, his unholstered revolver unsteady in his left hand.

"Don't bother, mister," the lead rider said. He yelled over his shoulder, "One of you go get the sheriff!"

Clayton let out his pent-up breath. "You jackass, I *am* the sheriff. At least until Calder's up and able."

"Is that right."

It wasn't a question. He assessed the trio of dusty riders on their lathered horses. "You must be the posse Calder mentioned."

"And you must be that Ranger fella we're lookin' for. You shot a man, left him to rot out on the north trail."

"Haven't been on the north trail. On any trail for the last two days." With slow, deliberate motions, he holstered his sidearm. No use riling up a bunch of men crazy for a capture. Someone could get hurt.

"You boys've got the wrong man."

"Oh, no we ain't," muttered a bulky rider attired incongruously in a mud-spattered three-piece suit. The tailor, no doubt. Clayton rolled his eyes. The tall, thin one with no hair must be Curly, the bartender at the Silver Swan. The third man had a beer belly that strained his shirt buttons. Must be a rich landowner with more ranch hands than he needed.

Clayton rested his palm lightly against his gun butt. He could take one of them if he had to—maybe two. But not all three. Not with his left hand, and not if he wanted to keep Irene safe. One of those trigger-drunk amateurs could accidentally send a stray bullet into her.

He eyed the apparent leader, whose horse danced nervously under his weight. It wasn't worth the risk. Very slowly he lifted his hand away from his gun. Then he turned his head and spoke quietly to Irene.

"Stay behind me and do what I say." He heard her low assent and then he spoke to the men.

"Let's go wake up the sheriff. When he's through laughing, we can all go home and get a good night's sleep. But first, the lady is going to cross the street behind me and walk up onto her front porch. We're all going to sit quiet until she's safe inside."

The fat rancher nodded. Clayton reached his good arm behind him until he felt the soft fabric of Irene's sleeve under his fingers. "Move," he ordered.

He felt her hesitate, then stiffen. "This," she whispered, "is the most upside-down evening of my life!"

"Mine, too. Now, move." He gave her a little shove and heard the swish of her skirt as she turned away. When her light, quick footsteps faded into silence, he addressed the posse.

"All right, gentlemen. I'm sure Sheriff Calder's waiting for whatever flapdoodle you're going to produce as your 'report.' Let's go."

It didn't work out anything like he thought it would. The posse tangled their stories together so bad no sane man could make sense of it. They'd found a rider...some gold dust in his pockets...been shot in the back...trail led toward town...figured it was that outlaw fella, Fortier and it was Black that killed him....

Sheriff Calder listened, but he didn't laugh. And then he turned a complete jelly-brained about-face and arrested Clayton for murder.

Chapter Eight

The clock on the courtroom wall tick-tick-ticked in the silence, broken only by the drone of a fly against the single-paned window. Clayton watched the creature bounce off the glass in its desperate quest for freedom. He knew the feeling. One minute he was acting sheriff of Crazy Creek, the next thing he knew Calder had turned the tables on him and arrested him. Now, two days later, he was on trial for murder. It made no sense.

"All rise," the portly bailiff yelled.

The onlookers surged off the plank benches and stood whispering among themselves in the sweltering July air. Clayton rose more deliberately, careful not to move his rebandaged shoulder. Every indrawn breath made his ribs hurt. Doc said he'd broken only two in the scuffle with the posse, but it felt like every bone above his belt buckle was on fire. Damn this town!

The bailiff lifted one leg and banged his boot heel against the whitewashed plank wall. "Order. Order in the court!" he bellowed.

A tall, gangly man tramped across the floor, his hands hidden in the folds of a rumpled black judicial robe. Unruly gray hair sprouted from his head in a thick, curly halo. Clayton thought he looked like an upended floor mop.

The judge mounted the single step to the bench, and the bailiff cleared his throat. "Circuit Judge Ransom Phipps presiding. All petitioners, witnesses 'n' spectators be seat—"

"All right, Jase, all right," the judge said in a weary voice. "I know you've been practicin' them fine words, but just plain old 'siddown' will do."

"Yessir, Yer Honor. Okay, ever'body, siddown!"

The crowd sank en masse onto the hard wooden seats.

"You, too, Mr. Black."

Clayton resumed his chair. Judge Phipps peered at him over the gold rims of his spectacles. "This the accused?"

The bailiff nodded. "Yessir. Name's Clayton Black, and he's a no-good horse-thievin' murderer!"

The judge thumped his gavel and the bailiff jerked.

"Control yourself, Jase. Trial's hardly started."

"Oh, sure. I mean, yessir, Yer Honor."

"Lawyer for the prosecution?" Phipps's gaze traveled over the crowded courtroom.

"Lawyer for the prosecution?" the bailiff repeated at the top of his lungs. Clayton winced at the volume of the man's voice.

A sharp-faced man stepped forward, clad in a dark suit so new the shelf creases still showed. Slightly too-short sleeves revealed two prominent wristbones and huge hands the color of chicken skin. "Martin Montgomery, Your Honor. Attorney-at-law residing in Cedarville, representing Morrow County."

Judge Phipps looked him up and down. "Mighty citified duds for a little hole-in-the-wall town like Crazy Creek," he observed mildly. "Still, I don't suppose it addles your brain none to look so beautiful."

A titter ran around the room, and the judge silenced it with a whack of his gavel. "Settle down, now. Lawyer for the defense?"

Clayton glanced at the clock. Twelve minutes after three. Irene said she'd help him, but first she had to make a trip to Cedarville. So where was she?

For the past three nights in his cell he'd told himself he didn't care about the outcome of this trial. Fortier was dead, and that's what mattered.

But right now he cared. He wanted a fair trial,

not some kangaroo court with a lynching party at the end.

"Lawyer for the defense?" the judge called again.

Silence. The clock ticked. The fly buzzed furiously in one corner of the window.

"Lawyer for the defense?" the bailiff bawled.

Sweat started to form between Clayton's shoulder blades. She'd deserted him. Right now he'd settle for anyone, experienced or raw, trained or not, as long as he walked through that door.

Once more Judge Phipps scanned the courtroom. "What attorney represents Mr....Black, is it?"

More silence. The clock hand jerked. Clayton's blue cavalry shirt began to stick to his skin.

"In that case," the judge began, his tone resigned, "we'll just—"

The door banged open. The first thing he saw was the top of a black silk parasol. Behind the parasol marched the young woman whose familiar, erect bearing and determined step reminded him that her spine was fashioned of wrought iron.

She lowered the parasol to one side and Clayton sucked in his breath. Smack on top of her upswept bun of dark chestnut hair rode That Hat. The one with the red cherries.

"Young woman," Judge Phipps said. "I don't suppose you're used to gettin' places on time, havin' to get all ladied up when you go out, but this here's a courtroom, and there's a trial goin' on.''

"Yes, I know," she responded in a clear voice. "I came as fast as I could, Your Honor."

"Then just take a seat, please, and we'll continue. Now, as I was sayin', since there's no lawyer representin' Mr. Black—"

Irene snapped her parasol shut. "I am representing Mr. Black."

Judge Phipps stared at her. Every man in the courtroom stared at her, Clayton noted. The women as well, but for different reasons, he'd wager. The women out of curiosity, the men out of, well, appreciation. He had to agree with them. She was pure woman. The rose-sprigged dress clung to her upper torso in a way that made his throat tighten.

He appreciated her, too—as a woman. But as a lawyer? *His* lawyer? By damn, he didn't know about that.

The bailiff and Lawyer Montgomery gaped at her. The judge ran a bony hand through his shock of gray curls. "You are—?"

"Irene Pennfield Hardisson," she announced in a clear, strong voice. "Attorney-at-law."

The judge's bushy gray brows waggled upward. "Have you any credentials, my dear?"

"Certainly," she snapped. She flicked open her reticule and removed a folded paper. It crackled as she spread it on the judge's broad desk. "Do not, please, refer to me as 'my dear.' Lawyer Hardisson or Miss Hardisson will do admirably."

Clayton suppressed a snort of laughter. Some nights ago she'd melted in his arms like warm honey. Today she was starched stiff as a corset stay.

"Of course, my d—Miss Hardisson." Judge Phipps adjusted his spectacles and inspected the document before him. "You came all the way from Philadelphia to defend this man?"

"Not exactly. I am here, however. And I do come from Philadelphia."

"Alone?"

"Of course. I have traveled alone since I was fifteen years old, and now I'm—never mind."

"Fifteen, eh?" The judge refolded the paper and handed it back to her. "Just where did you travel when you were fifteen, my d—Miss Hardisson?"

"To boarding school. And back. To college. And back. To—Your Honor, is this relevant?"

"Nope. Not the slightest. Interesting, though."

Clayton thought so, as well. More than interesting—unbelievable. He'd kissed her until he ached a few nights ago; now he felt as if he'd never laid eyes on her before.

"Your Honor, now that my credentials have been established, may I consult with my client in private?"

For the first time she turned to look at Clayton. The penetrating green eyes traveled over him as if he were a bug caught under a microscope. Once more he resisted the urge to stand up and smooth back his hair for inspection.

"Nope," the judge snapped. "He's charged with…lessee here, assault and battery. Horse thievin'. And if that isn't enough, he's accused of murder. I'm not lettin' him out of my sight. You can talk to him later. In his jail cell."

"I see." Her voice sounded controlled, but her eyes flashed green fire.

"Mr. Montgomery, as the prosecuting attorney, you want to add somethin'?"

The sharp-faced man tore his attention away from Irene and focused on the papers clutched in his hand. "Uh, no, Your Honor. I mean, yes! Mr. Black stands accused of murder."

"Already said that, son. Keep yer mind on her business."

Montgomery's angular face turned scarlet. Chuckles circled among the spectators, then bloomed into laughter.

Irene's voice cut through the noise. "Your Honor, I insist on a recess to consult with my client."

"Request denied."

"But—but Your Honor…"

"Don't 'but' me, Miss Hardisson. I'm the judge here, not you."

"Your Honor," she pursued. "May I—we—approach the bench?"

Lawyer Montgomery leaped eagerly to his feet. "Yes, may we?"

The judge motioned them forward. Clayton watched the rose-sprigged dress sway past him to the judge's bench. She lifted herself on tiptoe, spoke in whispers to the judge while her legal opponent gazed admiringly at her profile.

Clayton's damp shirt glued itself to the back of his chair. What the devil was she up to?

By the time he caught the drift, it was too late. The judge rapped his gavel and both lawyers took their places behind the battered oak table that served as the bar.

His trial was under way.

Irene closed the door to the sheriff's office, expelling her breath when she heard the click of the latch. Dust motes danced in the sunlight slanting across the worn plank floor. It was nearly four o'clock; court had adjourned until nine the following morning, which meant she could confer with Clayton for an hour before taking dinner at the Maybud Hotel and then spend the evening preparing her presentation for tomorrow.

She advanced two steps toward the scarred oak

desk where the dozing sheriff slumped. "Sheriff Calder?"

The man's graying head drooped toward his belly, his chin grazing the top button of his faded blue-checked shirt. Other than his breath wheezing in and out, there wasn't a sound.

"Excuse me, Mr. Calder. I want to see—"

"Come on back, ma'am," a quiet voice interrupted. "The sheriff, there, has had a hard day waltzin' me to and from the courtroom. Plumb wore him out."

"Clayton? Is that you?"

"It is. Nobody back here but me, and I'm behind bars. You're safe."

Irene straightened and tiptoed past the sheriff's desk. A puff of warm, stale air wafted through the arched opening in the adobe wall. It smelled faintly of scorched beans and mildew, and she wrinkled her nose.

"Doesn't pay to breathe too deep. Only thing worse than the air in here is the food."

Irene scanned the two shadowy iron-barred cells. One was empty. In the other Clayton lay stretched out on a cot, one arm folded over his eyes.

She hesitated. "Clayton, you have to talk to me. I am your attorney."

"Like hell you are." He made no move to rise.

"I most certainly am," Irene retorted.

"You're the last thing I need, Irene. I got

enough problems in this civilized hellhole you
think so much of to last me a lifetime—a woman
is more than I can handle right now.''

"Nevertheless," she responded, her voice cool,
"I am going to defend you." She'd grabbed the
chance as soon as she heard about the murder
charge. She would win this case and the news
would travel all the way to Portland. Her reputation
in Oregon would be firmly established, and—most
important of all—she would save the life of a man
she had come to value.

"I'm the best lawyer in town," she continued.
"In fact, I'm the only lawyer in town, unless you
want to try to sober up Lysander Pettigrew at the
Silver Swan saloon."

He digested her words. "I figure you can get by
on charm for about ten minutes out here. After that,
you'd better know something."

"I know something," she assured him. "May I
come in?"

"Get the key," he said, his tone resigned. "On
the hook by the window."

My, what a lackadaisical way to run a jail! She
retrieved the round iron ring, selected one of the
two knobby keys and jabbed it into the lock. The
cell door grated open. He didn't move a muscle.

"If this is an inconvenient time, I could come
back after supp—"

"Not inconvenient," his low voice drawled. "Just a waste of time."

Irene blinked. *A waste of time?* The man was on trial for his life and speaking to his lawyer was a waste of time?

She stepped into the cell.

"Sit up," she ordered. "I've come to help you."

"What makes you think you can? This is a setup if I ever saw one."

"Perhaps. In which case I will prove that is so."

"Wild-goose chase," he muttered. His black lashes swept up to reveal steady gray eyes boring into hers. "I've been beat up and thrown in jail before. I know what happens to…people like me who don't fit in."

"Nonsense. That's why we have the Constitution. Judges and juries. And lawyers. Do you mind if I sit down?"

"Nope. Suit yourself." His gaze indicated a battered three-legged stool at the foot of his cot. She dragged it forward and settled herself on the hard wooden seat. She was seeing another side of Clayton Black. Lord, the man had more layers than Nora's fold-over pastry! And not all of them were tender.

He raised the upper part of his torso into a sitting position and swung his booted feet onto the floor, groaning with the effort. His blue canvas shirt was bloodstained.

Irene frowned. "You're accused of killing Brance Fortier. Is that true?"

"It's true that I'm accused. I didn't kill him, though."

"You knew the man, however."

"Yep. Like I told you, been trackin' him for more than a year. Slippery son of a gun."

He leveled a steel-eyed gaze on her. "And when I caught up with him, I was to take him back to Texas or shoot him, whichever came first."

Irene flinched. "I advise you not to repeat that in court, about planning to shoot Mr. Fortier."

"Yeah?" Again, a grin twitched across the fine mouth. "Just what the hell difference will it make? I tracked him through Colorado and Montana, planned how I was gonna take him back to Allenville with me, ridin' or trussed on a packhorse in an oilskin shroud. So now he turns up dead and the posse claims I did it. I don't figure there's a way in hell you can get me out of this."

"Clayton, let me worry about that."

"Waste of time," he murmured.

Stung, Irene drilled him with a look. "I am not a waste of time. I, and my father before me, never lost a single case back in Philadelphia, and I don't intend to start now."

"How many murder cases you try back in Philadelphia?"

Oh, the man was maddening! "Well, I…actually, I handled more financial matters than murders. But I excelled at reading law and am well qualified to practice before this or any other bar. Besides, it strikes me you don't have a choice. I've decided to defend you, and defend you I will!"

Lazily he lifted his good arm, palm up, and leaned back against the gray adobe wall. "Yeah." His tone betrayed his disbelief.

Irene thought hard for a few moments while the sheriff snored in the outer room and a sparrow chirped sporadically outside the single small cell window. She wasn't sure how to deal with this side of Clayton Black. He was remote. Full of anger.

"We'll start with your gun," she announced, working to keep her voice calm. She drew a pencil and notepad from her reticule.

"Sheriff's got my sidearm locked up. Rifle was on my horse."

"What kind of ammunition do you use?"

"For the revolver, forty-five Colt."

She nodded. "Where is your horse now?"

"Damned if I know."

"Would you recognize it if you saw it again?"

He gave her a long, steady look. "A man out

here might forget a bartender, a hotel clerk, even a woman. But not his horse. Black gelding with a white slash on his face. Smart. Name's Rebel.''

"And the rifle?"

"Winchester. Gift from my father—got his initials carved on the stock. JB. Josh Black.''

She scribbled on the notepad.

"You grew up in Texas?" It was a routine question, but when he didn't answer, she looked up and caught her breath. The gray eyes had hardened into stone.

"You already know that."

"Your mother?"

"Her name was Mariette Varlon.''

"And your father?"

"I told you, Fortier killed him.''

Startled at the fury she sensed under his words, Irene stared at him. He might appear relaxed, even nonchalant, as if he didn't care one way or the other about the outcome of his trial, but she'd hit a vulnerable spot with the question about his mother. There was much more to this man below the surface, and he kept it well hidden. A sixth sense told her the layers went deep and sheltered great pain.

Any sane man in his position would be squirming with impatience or at least unease. Clayton seemed almost disinterested in his fate, and that bothered her. It didn't make sense.

The challenge intrigued her. And the man, as well. This was why she'd come out West in the first place, wasn't it? To be involved in real life, things that mattered?

Things like life and death. Like Clayton Black's trial for murder.

Like Clayton Black, the man.

Clayton settled himself back on the iron cot, stretched out his long, jean-clad legs, and folded his good arm to cushion the back of his head. Without speaking, he watched Irene smooth her skirt and turn toward the cell door.

Amazing creatures, women. Just when you think you understand them, they do something that sets your head spinning.

She wasn't dumb, he knew that. But he did question her good judgment. She might know law, but she sure didn't know criminals. Any outlaw with half a brain would have wrestled those keys away from her and escaped without so much as a by-your-leave.

And another thing—another woman would wring her hands or cry at the fix he was in. But Irene just sat herself down on that stool and peppered him with questions.

The cell door whined open and he heard the rustle of petticoats.

"Is there anything you want?" her crisp voice asked. The door clanged shut.

Clayton's lids snapped open. "What?"

"I'll try to see to your needs while you're in jail," she explained. "Is there something you're lacking?"

"Besides my right arm and my freedom, you mean?" *Besides a woman?*

He didn't mean to sound so gruff. The truth was she'd about wore his throat raw answering her questions the past hour.

A little frown creased the smooth area between her dark eyebrows. "Of course, your freedom," she echoed. "It does seem…unusual for someone in your position to be so cavalier about being on trial for murder."

"Maybe that's because a part of me doesn't much care anymore." He surprised himself by the admission, especially to her. He'd never shared much of himself with a woman before. What he said next surprised him even more.

"What I set out to do has been accomplished. Fortier's dead. That's all the outcome I've been thinking about."

She drew in a long, slow breath and expelled it

in a whoosh through pursed lips. "What will happen to you after the trial?"

He noticed that she watched his face steadily, her green eyes measuring him as if trying to decide whether one side of his face matched the other.

After. The word rattled around in his brain like a piece of loose grapeshot. He hadn't thought about *after.* He'd only thought about "when" and "how." For two days he'd lain on this cot, deadening the pain in his cracked ribs with Sheriff Calder's bad whiskey, feeling a hollow relief in his gut.

It was over. A year of tracking through dust storms, across mountain passes with snow so thick he couldn't see his hand in front of his face, up steep-sided canyons and through rivers. And then someone else had cornered his quarry and killed him. He guessed it didn't matter. Fortier was dead, and that was all he'd cared about.

He wrenched his thoughts away from Pa and Jannie. He'd wanted revenge. Now he felt empty.

"Haven't thought much about 'after,'" he said. "But, seein' as you're askin', there is something I'd purely like to have right now."

Her gaze moved from his jaw to his eyes. "And what is that?"

"A decent cup of coffee."

And one night, just one night, in her arms.

* * *

Irene jerked the key out of the lock and hung the ring back on its nail. *Coffee!* Was the man out of his mind? Incarcerated in a hot, smelly jail cell for almost a week and all he wanted was coffee? Not a bath or a Bible or writing paper to contact his mother or even to make out a will? Didn't he realize the judge could hang him?

She stomped into the outer office, sweeping between the sheriff's desk and the potbellied stove.

"Wh—huh?" Sheriff Calder lurched out of his seat. "Oh, it's you, Miss Hardisson. Come to see the prisoner, didja?" He scratched his belly with one huge hand.

"Came, saw and am now taking my leave," she pronounced. "Good afternoon, Sheriff."

"Well, I'll be—"

She shut the door on the man's sputtering and headed for the Maybud Hotel and supper. Something didn't add up. Clayton seemed resigned, as if he had not one iota of interest in the fact that he was accused of murder.

"Well," she huffed as she sailed along the board walkway. "My work is cut out for me, that's plain to see."

At the hotel, she scanned the menu. Steak. Pork chops. Beans and bacon. Biscuits.

The first thing she ordered was a pot of hot cof-

fee, to be delivered to the jail. The last thing she
ordered was a thick steak and a basket of biscuits.
She'd have to work all night to prepare her case
for trial.

Chapter Nine

Irene lifted her head from the table where she'd fallen asleep. Mornings in Oregon were noisier than they were in Philadelphia. Scores of birds chattered outside her bedroom window, and blinding gold sunlight poured over the papers on her makeshift desk.

She'd spent half the night studying the notes she'd made at Moody's Undertaking in Cedarville and the other half planning her strategy. Now it was eight o'clock; she had barely an hour to wash, dress, eat breakfast, and outline her opening arguments for the morning court session.

She gathered up her notes and began stripping off her clothes for a quick wash. Her back ached and her eyes, swollen and grainy from lack of sleep, kept drifting shut.

She settled her hat atop her smoothed-back chestnut hair, pinned her father's gold watch to the yoke of her blue-striped cambric dress, and gathered up her leather satchel and her black lace parasol. Giving her face a final check in the dresser mirror as she passed, she opened the door and resolutely trod down the stairs.

''All rise!'' the bailiff bellowed.

Clayton watched the spectators surge to their feet, the jury members whispering among themselves until shushed by the burly man framed in the doorway. Stiff from a night spent trying to find a comfortable position with two new broken ribs and the old bullet wound in his shoulder, he used the edge of the counsel table he shared with Irene to heave himself to his feet.

At his right, his lawyer swayed on her tiny black kid shoes, then steadied herself by jabbing the tip of her parasol into the plank floor. The bright fruit on her hat trembled until Judge Phipps seated himself behind the bench.

She was a picture, Clayton thought. But great balls of fire, could a woman that pretty really be a capable attorney?

Last night he'd worked to convince himself it didn't matter whether she lost the case—Fortier was dead. What happened to him, personally, was secondary. The only thing he regretted was that he'd never solve the mystery of this contradictory female.

But today when he stepped into the cramped, stifling room that served as a courtroom, Clayton's every instinct reminded him he was alive and he preferred to stay that way. In court, his gut agitated for freedom. But in his jail cell at night, reflecting on his boyhood in Texas, his life as a half-breed Cherokee passing for white, his logical mind argued for acceptance of the situation.

At least for the time being. He was too beat-up to ride hard right now; his best bet was to gamble that she was right about this supposedly civilized law-and-order town and its fair-minded jury. He'd chosen to stay and face his accusers with his eyes wide-open.

Now, facing that sharp-eyed, craggy-faced judge and the hungry-looking jury members, his instinct for self-preservation tightened his chest.

He'd always suspected that some Indian hater would do him in one of these days. He'd take responsibility for his actions like the next man, but he didn't want to die for something he *didn't* do. If it came to that, he'd—

Judge Phipps rapped for order. "Court's in session," he barked.

Irene resumed her seat and leaned toward him. "We're pleading not guilty," she intoned.

A subtle fragrance rose from her hair. Lilacs. The scent drove a knife into his heart. His momma had loved flowers, lilacs especially. Every April he could recall, clouds of lavender blooms graced the front porch posts. She'd brought the cuttings with her from New Orleans when she'd married Pa.

In spite of himself, Clayton breathed in the heady, sweet smell. If he closed his eyes, he could see the ranch house, and remember.

"Mr. Black?" the judge rasped. "How do you plead?"

Irene rose. Her petticoats brushed against his calf, and another puff of scented air wafted upward. Clayton's throat closed over a lump the size of an orange.

"Your Honor, my client pleads not guilty."

The prosecuting attorney leaped to his feet. "Not guilty! Why, that's preposterous!" His Adam's apple worked above his shirt collar, his thin neck beginning to flush. "Prepos—"

The gavel cut him off. "Heard you the first time, son," the judge said in a tired voice. "Prisoner's presumed innocent until proven guilty. You'll get your chance. Now, siddown!"

Clayton folded his hands on the table before him and studied his thumbs. It would be easy—too easy—to link him to Fortier's murder. Lawyer or no, the minute they found out he was a half-breed, he wouldn't stand a chance.

Irene sat upright in the chair beside him, her spine straight as a poker. In her gauzy dress with that decorated red hat, she looked like a stalk of Indian paintbrush.

"Your Honor, my investigation into this matter has yielded evidence which proves my client's innocence." She unbuckled the leather satchel and drew out a piece of paper. "In the first place—"

"You, too, missy," Judge Phipps growled. "This here court operates legal-like. Prosecution's first. You wait your turn."

"But Your Honor, I can prove—"

"Not yet, you can't. Bailiff, swear in the prisoner."

Clayton watched her chin come up and her hands close into fists as the bailiff ambled forward. He stepped to meet him, placed his right hand on the proffered Bible and swore to tell the truth.

But he didn't look at the bailiff. Instead, he watched his lawyer, seated at the table next to his empty chair. As he spoke the words, her gaze met his and held, and something kicked him in the pit of his stomach.

She looked cool and calm in her soft blue-striped dress. In spite of her diminutive size, she was almost regal with that challenging look in her eyes. All five feet of her made him uneasy, and she was looking back at him like he might have his hat on backward or forgot to button up his trousers. Her eyes were green as Texas grass in the spring. He liked the way the dark pupils widened and narrowed as her mind chewed on something. He hoped that look would unnerve Lawyer Montgomery. It sure as hell did something to his own insides.

Irene watched her client lower his rangy frame into the witness chair and face the prosecuting attorney. Clayton crossed one ankle over the other and stretched his long legs out in front of him. He looked oddly relaxed for a man on trial for killing someone. Now that she knew he hadn't done it, she thought she understood his attitude. He trusted her to prove his innocence.

She'd do better than that. She'd have the murder charge dropped by this afternoon.

Lawyer Montgomery quick-stepped toward the witness stand. "Now then, Mr. Black. You're from Texas, I understand. And you've been away about a year. I suppose there's a good reason for that." He twirled a strand of his mustache around and around his index finger and waited.

"You askin' or tellin'?" Clayton replied.

Irene pricked up her ears. Her client sounded surly. She hadn't advised him on courtroom demeanor, merely assumed that any intelligent man would be polite and cooperative, under the circumstances.

"Well, uh, I'm asking, of course. That's my job as prosecuting attorney, asking the questions. Your task—under oath, I remind you—is to answer them.'' He leaned back expectantly.

The silence stretched until Irene wanted to scream. She tried to catch Clayton's eye, but he looked resolutely at the floor or out the side window where two or three horses stood tethered to the hitching rail. Everywhere but at her. Finally he grinned and recrossed his legs.

''Well, I'm waitin'. What's the question?''

Lawyer Montgomery's pinstripe-swathed arm jerked. ''The question, Mr. Black, is—if you call Texas home, what are you doing out here in Oregon?''

''Right now, I'm eatin' bad grub and lettin' a couple of ribs that half-assed posse busted get better.''

A perplexed look crossed the attorney's narrow face.

''Answer the question, son,'' the judge directed. ''What were you doing out here in the first place?''

Clayton hesitated. ''Trackin' a man.''

The prosecutor brightened. ''And what man was that, Mr. Black?''

''Name's Fortier.''

''Aha!'' The prosecutor practically twitched with excitement. ''So you actually knew Mr. Fortier, the man who was shot?''

Irene forced herself to swallow. *Don't admit too much,* she silently willed her client.

"Yep. Knew his name and the look of him. His manner of travelin', that sort of thing."

Good! Irene mentally commanded him to look at her for cues. Instead, he stared into the watery blue eyes of the prosecuting attorney.

"Did you know Mr. Fortier back in Texas?"

Clayton took his time answering. "In a manner of speakin'. I trailed him from Texas. But it started in New Orleans."

Irene sat up straighter. *Careful. Don't volunteer any information. Make the prosecution work for it!*

Lawyer Montgomery's pale eyes lit up. "*It?* Just what 'it' was it that started in New Orleans?"

Clayton's tongue came out to wet his lips. Irene clenched her palms in her lap. "Objection," she called. "Irrelevant. Question has no discernible purpose."

"Overruled," the judge snapped. "Tell us 'bout New Orleans, Mr. Black. I've never been there myself."

"Objection! Your Honor, if I may point out—"

"Overruled." He leaned forward, his eyes avid. "Now, son, tell us."

For the first time, her client sent her a quick look. Irene could swear his normally cool gray eyes shone with amusement. Why, he was playing with them! Just like a cat in a nest of mice.

"N'Orleans is beautiful. Beautiful houses, sugar plantations, steamboats, beautiful women—"

Judge Phipps caught his breath. "Tell us 'bout the women," he said softly.

Oh, for Lord's sake, Irene thought. Her client was purposely trailing a red herring under the judge's nose so he could steer interest away from what had happened in New Orleans. Which, she acknowledged, must be what he'd told her that night they had played Truth Poker. About Fortier killing his father and sister.

For the first time in her professional life, she sat back and watched her client—an accused murderer—ably throw the prosecution, even the judge, off the track. He was like a chameleon. He kept changing his words, even his personality, to suit the moment.

And then she bristled. Just who did he think he was, anyway? That was *her* job!

"Well," Clayton said, taking his time over the word. "There's two kinds of women in N'Orleans...."

Every man in the room drew in his breath and held it. The few women sprinkled among them sniffed and pressed their lips into a line. Irene noted the flush of color on Lawyer Montgomery's cheeks.

"The first kind," Clayton continued, his voice lazy, "is a lady. The other kind...isn't."

"You have much, uh, knowledge of the other kind, son?"

"Some," Clayton admitted.

Sighs like wind through pine trees echoed among the male spectators. Irene frowned. Things were getting out of hand.

"Your Honor, this line of questioning has gone quite far enough!"

Lawyer Montgomery ran a bony finger under his starched shirt collar. "I quite agree with my learned opponent, Your Honor. This is not the proper place to discuss, um, loose women."

That brought a spatter of applause from the ladies.

Judge Phipps banged his gavel. "On the contrary, Mr. Montgomery. If you'd been on your toes in prosecuting this man, you would have seen the point. As it is, you got me doing your thinking for you."

The prosecuting attorney opened his mouth, then closed it. "Oh. Oh, yes. Thank you, Your—"

Judge Phipps ignored him. "Something happened in New Orleans that made you light out after Fortier, is that it?"

Clayton sat silent.

"Answer the question, by damn! This here's a courtroom!"

Irene stood up. "Your Honor, I can prove—"

The gavel cut her off. "Something to do with a woman, maybe?"

"Maybe."

"Yes or no," the judge barked.

"Yes," came her client's low answer.

Instant silence descended. Irene felt her stomach clench. Why, oh why did he suddenly decide to give a straight answer? He was succeeding brilliantly in leading both the prosecuting attorney and the judge on a wild-goose chase. Why stop now? In exasperation she stared at the man she hoped to defend.

She was struck by the change in his face. The stony gray eyes had softened, and his gaze was not on the floor but focused on something beyond the window. The hard mouth gentled.

And then the dark lashes swept down for an instant and he turned his face away, as if to escape something. In that moment, Irene knew he must not say one word more. Judge Phipps had unknowingly uncovered the connection—a motivation for murder. She had to stop the questioning.

Immediately.

"Your Honor," she demanded. "I request a short recess to—"

"Denied."

"But—"

"I said denied!" The judge cut her off with a flourish of his gavel. His black eyes snapped.

Oh, no! This could not continue. She had to do something! But the judge wouldn't let her speak a complete sentence, much less acknowledge her objections. The situation called for drastic action.

Across the room she caught Clayton watching her, his eyes expressionless. It didn't matter. She'd seen the pain in them, knew what he was hiding. As his attorney, she had to protect him.

"Mr. Black?" the judge prompted.

Irene made her decision. Stepping out from behind the desk, she moved toward Judge Phipps. When she was three feet from the bench, she lifted one hand to her forehead, uttered a small cry and managed to sink to the floor in a cloud of blue cambric.

Chapter Ten

Irene coughed and opened her eyes as the vial of lavender salts passed under her nose a third time. She looked up into the bailiff's round, concerned face.

"You all right, ma'am?"

"Yes, thank you." She tried to sit up, but the large hand on her shoulder prevented it.

"Let me up, please."

"Judge said to watch over you. Cleared the courtroom, he did, and most of 'em is outside now for a smoke or a dipper of water. It's awful hot in here, ma'am. Judge figgered you might like to loosen your…"

His face turned scarlet.

"Certainly not." She was healthy as a young colt. A couple of hours in a warm courtroom was nothing new to her. Besides, she hadn't really fainted; she was just a good actress.

"I am perfectly all right, thank you. Now, let me up."

A tall figure moved into the doorway. "I'd do what the lady asks if I were you," a low voice said.

Irene looked up into Clayton's hard gray eyes. He moved toward the bailiff in a slow, easy walk, but as he neared she saw his lips thin and his hands fold into two rocklike fists.

"Now," Clayton said quietly. "I don't give second warnings."

The bailiff scooted his bulky frame backward until his spine met a chair. His hands scrabbled on the wooden seat and then he hoisted himself to his feet and edged sideways out of the courtroom.

"You all right?" Her client loomed over her.

"Quite," she replied as steadily as she could.

"I expected you'd be half-sozzled on those smelling salts by now." The smallest hint of a smile tugged at his mouth.

"I tried not to breathe in," she confessed.

"Why'd you do it?"

Irene stood up and brushed off her skirt. "Why? To stop you from saying too much, that's why! You and I need to confer before court resumes."

Quickly she explained her strategy and told him to stop volunteering information. He just looked at her with calm, tired eyes.

Clayton gazed down at her flushed, heart-shaped

face and a flicker of warmth curled into his chest. He almost felt sorry for her, going to the trouble of "fainting" so she could warn him. She was conscientious, he'd say that for her. But a bit unorthodox. And bullheaded.

"Maybe you don't see it like I do," he offered. "Maybe you're fighting a losing battle."

Irene bit her lip. "I am the attorney here, not you. Let me do the thinking so I can save your life."

Clayton blinked. This delicate, ruffly creature was going to save him? Not likely. Why, a good gust of wind would blow her onto her backside. He had to chuckle at the thought.

Not even remotely possible, considering he'd actually wanted Fortier dead. That'd be plenty of motive for most juries.

"Clayton?"

Persistent, too. Hell, she'd never shut up unless he stuffed something into her craw to chew on.

"Fortier was my mother's half brother."

"Her brother! You mean he—he was your own uncle?"

"He was. I tracked him because I wanted revenge. I wanted to kill him." He spoke the words without inflection, worked to keep talking over the ache in his throat.

"But—" She stopped abruptly and peered up at him.

People began streaming through the doorway, thumping chairs, talking. *"Court will now resume!"* The bailiff's raucous voice grated on Irene's nerves. The scent of cigarette smoke hung on the hot, still air.

"Clayton," she whispered urgently. "Listen to me. I can prove you could not—"

"All rise!"

"Oh, bother," she moaned. "Just trust me," she hissed up at him as the crowd flowed around them. "Don't divulge..."

She was swept away by a knot of onlookers. Clayton watched her regain her chair and her composure—to a degree. Her cheeks were still reddened, her dark, arched eyebrows drawn together in a frown. She flashed him a last look before the judge strode to his place behind the bench, and his heart slammed into his ribs.

He would remember that look of trust and confidence in him all the rest of his life.

He turned away. If he *had* a life.

Lawyer Montgomery rubbed his bony hands together. "Do I understand that you carried a grudge against this Fortier fellow?" Sweat stood out on his high forehead.

Understandable, Irene thought. It had taken him an hour and a quarter to extract this much information. Clayton made the prosecuting attorney work hard for every fact.

"I did," Clayton replied.

"And you planned to kill him when you caught up with him," the lawyer observed. He turned to the jury.

"Gentlemen, you see before you the perpetrator of a premeditated, cold-blooded murder."

"Objection!" Irene said in a tired voice. "That has not yet been established beyond a reasonable doubt."

"Overruled." Judge Phipps waved a listless hand at her. "I'm getting mighty tired of these continual objections, young woman."

Irene stiffened her backbone and rose from her chair. "Well, Your Honor, I am growing weary of voicing them! If you would just take the time to listen—"

"Denied," the judge interjected. "Get back to the grudge, Mr. Montgomery."

Oh! She would explode any minute. If she bit her tongue any harder, she would draw blood. All she needed was five minutes to present her evidence, and then the charges would be dismissed and they could all go home.

"So," the prosecutor continued, "you shot him in the back. Just like you planned."

Clayton's face darkened. "Never in my life have

I shot a man in the back. When I shot one, it was head-on.''

"*When?* Did you say *when* you shot him? Then there isn't a shred of doubt that you did just that!''

"Objec—''

Crack went the gavel. "Overruled.''

It was like a ritual, Irene thought. She opened her mouth and Judge Phipps banged that gavel down. The hot, still air in the courtroom pressed down on her as the clock clicked away the minutes. Lawyer Montgomery's plodding, tedious examination would never end.

An hour passed, then another, and still the prosecutor fumbled his way along, drawing bits of incriminating testimony from her client. Judge Phipps's eyelids drooped. Two of the women fanned themselves with folded copies of the *Crazy Creek Reader* they'd bought during the noon recess.

Irene eyed the headline. Murderer On Trial. The subhead made her stomach lurch. Lumber Needed For Gallows.

She felt hot and sticky and out of sorts. What she wouldn't give for a cool bath! Or at least an end to Montgomery's interminable examination of her client. Of the two, neither seemed likely to occur in the next three hours.

If only there were a way to hurry up the prosecution! Unfortunately, she realized as she watched her opponent posture and preen before the jury and the spectators, Lawyer Montgomery was enjoying the limelight so much he might never end his exhibition!

She couldn't faint again; she'd already done that. She settled back against the hard oak chair and set her mind to another task—how to abort Lawyer Montgomery's future appearances before the jury.

All at once she heard the prosecuting attorney's thin voice. "Your witness, Miss Hardisson."

At last! Irene dug into her satchel and pulled out two small, handkerchief-wrapped bundles. With careful fingers, she untied the knot of the first one, dumped the contents into the palm of her hand and moved to face her client.

"Mr. Black, if you were to shoot a man, any man, what kind of weapon would you use?"

Clayton blinked in surprise. "A rifle."

"Do you own a rifle?"

"Sure. A Winchester."

"And what caliber bullet does it use?"

He quirked one eyebrow. "Thirty-thirties."

Irene turned toward the jury, taking care to make eye contact with each man as she spoke. "I have in my hand two bullets, removed from the back of the deceased by Mr. Moody, the undertaker in Cedarville, where the body was taken.'' She tipped her palm to expose the two pieces of metal.

''Gentlemen?'' She moved nearer and passed her hand under the gazes of the jury members. ''What size bullets are these?''

Heads bent. Spectacles were adjusted.

''By Gawd,'' a lanky, sandy-haired rancher breathed. ''They're forty-fives. Lookit, Jack,'' he said to the man next to him. ''Them's forty-five-caliber bullets!''

Irene smiled at him. ''Exactly. Revolver bullets. I compliment your acute observation.''

The rancher expanded visibly under her praise.

''What is obvious to this man should by now be apparent to all of you. These bullets did not come from Clayton Black's rifle. In fact, a rifle was not used in the slaying.''

A rustle of whispers swept the courtroom. Irene stepped away from the jury and turned to hold her client's gaze. ''So you see, ladies and gentleman, you have brought the wrong man to trial. Mr. Black is none other than the son of the well-known and highly respected Texas Ranger Josh Black. He is not a murderer.''

More murmurs.

''In fact,'' Irene continued, looking from Lawyer Montgomery's startled gaze to Judge Phipps's now wide-awake countenance, ''Clayton Black is himself a Texas Ranger. He was tracking Mr. Fortier because Fortier was an outlaw, a murderer. But Mr. Black's intent was to capture, not to kill. Someone else pulled the trigger that day—not my client.''

The judge's gavel quieted the outburst that followed. When silence returned, Judge Phipps leaned forward. ''What have you got in that other hanky, Miss Hardisson?''

Irene replaced the first exhibit and dumped the contents of the second bundle into her palm. ''This is the bullet Dr. Martin in Cedarville dug out of Mr. Black's shoulder the day he was brought into that town.''

She returned to the jury, and this time addressed the sandy-haired rancher directly. ''Can you identify this bullet?''

He bobbed his head over her hand, then straightened. ''Slug from a thirty-thirty,'' he announced. He beamed at his fellow jurors. ''Rifle bullet.''

Irene closed her fingers around the metal pieces. ''And that, gentlemen, means that Clayton Black did not kill Mr. Fortier. Mr. Fortier, I'm sure you remember, was shot in the back. By a revolver.''

''Gol-dangit! Black must be innocent,'' someone in the crowd muttered into the sudden hush.

Lawyer Montgomery looked as if he'd been poleaxed. ''But...but surely—''

How to validate your
Editor's FREE GIFT "Thank You"

1. Peel off gift seal from front cover. Place it in space provided at right. This automatically entitles you to receive 2 FREE BOOKS and a fabulous mystery gift.

2. Send back this card and you'll get 2 brand-new Harlequin Historicals® novels. These books have a cover price of $4.99 each in the U.S. and $5.99 each in Canada, but they are yours to keep absolutely free.

3. There's no catch. You're under no obligation to buy anything. We charge nothing—ZERO—for your first shipment. And you don't have to make any minimum number of purchases—not even one!

4. The fact is, thousands of readers enjoy receiving their books by mail from the Harlequin Reader Service®. They enjoy the convenience of home delivery...they like getting the best new novels at discount prices BEFORE they're available in stores...and they love their *Heart to Heart* subscriber newsletter featuring author news, horoscopes, recipes, book reviews and much more!

5. We hope that after receiving your free books you'll want to remain a subscriber. But the choice is yours— to continue or cancel, any time at all! So why not take us up on our invitation, with no risk of any kind. You'll be glad you did!

6. Don't forget to detach your FREE BOOKMARK. And remember...just for validating your Editor's Free Gift Offer, we'll send you THREE gifts, *ABSOLUTELY FREE!*

GET A FREE MYSTERY GIFT...

YOURS FREE!

SURPRISE MYSTERY GIFT COULD BE YOURS **FREE** AS A SPECIAL "THANK YOU" FROM THE EDITORS OF HARLEQUIN

Visit us online at
www.eHarlequin.com

"Order!" Judge Phipps's gavel barked. "Miss Hardisson?"

"Your Honor?" Irene replied as sweetly as she could.

"Approach the bench!"

Chapter Eleven

Judge Phipps leaned over the rough plank desk that served as a judge's bench and glared at Irene. "Now you look here, missy. Are you askin' us to believe that Clayton Black is innocent?"

Irene met the judge's snapping dark eyes. "I am."

"And you say the proof is in those bullets you got tied up in your lacy hankies?"

Irene smiled at the old man. She had—finally!—gotten his attention. "Exactly, Your Honor. The evidence is there in cold, hard metal."

"Hogwash! First off, you got to get this Cedarville doctor and the undertaker in here to swear those slugs are what you say they are. Otherwise, missy, a pretty lady like you might try to hoodwink a jury into believin' just about anything you wanted 'em to!"

Fury surged through her. The judge was prejudiced against her simply because she was a woman! "Your Honor, I assure you—"

"That's all, Lawyer Hardisson."

Her heart sank. She'd hoped to have the charges against her client dismissed, but at bottom, she knew the judge was right. Now she'd have to convince her two witnesses to testify and have them summoned into court. Then there would no doubt be more hours wasted while Lawyer Montgomery completed his circuitous cross-examinations. The case against Clayton Black could be completed by tomorrow were it not for Judge Phipps!

In spite of herself, she respected the judge's insistence on proper courtroom procedure. Oh, all right, she would do it his way, she decided. Anything to get her client acquitted. No doubt the minute he was free, he would head back to Texas. She knew exactly where she would go—home to wallpaper her bedroom.

"Very well, Your Honor. Please subpoena Dr. Randolph Martin and Seamus Moody, the undertaker in Cedarville."

"Don't give me orders, missy," the judge growled. "I see what needs t'be done. Jase!" he barked.

The bailiff jerked awake at the sound of his name. He surged out of his chair and stood at attention, swaying on his feet. "Yessir?"

"Ride on over to Cedarville and tell Doc Martin

and Seamus Moody t'be here tomorrow. Ten o'clock. Sober,'' he added.

The bailiff hesitated, then shook his head. "Cain't do that, Judge. I hear Doc Martin's gone to Weed Junction to visit his sister, and Seamus is down with the grippe.''

"You mean he's drunk,'' Judge Phipps asserted.

"Nope. He's sick, right enough. 'Bout puked his guts out, beggin' yer pardon, ma'am.''

Irene's spirits drooped even lower. Another delay. Another restless night with nothing to occupy her mind but how frustrated she felt. *And lonely,* a voice added.

On the surface, she maintained the cool, controlled manner that had been bred into her, but inside, when she was by herself, she came face-to-face with her real feelings. She cared more than she should about what happened to Clayton Black. And that, she acknowledged, frightened her more than her first murder trial!

She needed to keep moving, keep her mind active so she could hold her unease in check.

"Your Honor, how long will it take—''

"Couple a' days, missy. You'd best take up your knittin' to keep yourself amused.''

"Knitting!'' Irene recoiled.

"My wife says it sure makes the time fly,'' the judge said, his voice softening.

Irene couldn't tell if he was smiling. His bushy mustache drooped over his mouth.

She let her shoulders sag in defeat.

Knitting? The very idea! Why, her father would spin in his grave at the prospect! Would the most learned attorney in Philadelphia approve of a daughter who…knitted?

The judge waved her away from the bench. "Court will recess until day after tomorrow, ten o'clock." The gavel cracked against the judge's oak tabletop.

Irene sank into the chair next to Clayton. Perhaps a card game…

It would give her something to do, something to think about besides her client.

She released a long sigh and in the next instant straightened her spine and sent a sideways glance at Clayton, his long body folded into the chair beside her. He held her gaze, an odd amusement dancing in his gray eyes.

He was not just her client, she reflected. He was the man whose lips had seared hers with unspoken emotion.

Quelling the little flutter in her belly, she leaned toward him. "Would you," she whispered behind her hand, "like to play a set of poker?"

Clayton leaned back against the cool adobe wall behind his cot and studied the young woman across from him. She'd brought a whole pot of hot coffee from the Maybud Hotel dining room, and he appreciated that. But she sure was out of place.

She looked too delicate to be sitting here in a jail cell. She was a lady, an educated lady at that. Why was she spending her time playing a "set" of poker with him? In spite of himself, he smiled at her choice of words.

"Deal the cards," he ordered. He tried not to chuckle at her delight.

She leaned across the makeshift table—an upended wooden cracker barrel—shuffled the deck awkwardly, and presented it for cutting. "Shall we play Truth Poker?"

Clayton blinked. All at once he thought of a hundred reasons why he shouldn't be doing this.

The night air hung heavy and still. Over the sound of their breathing in the close, squalid cell came the faint sound of a fiddle playing a slow waltz.

All of a sudden he couldn't breathe. The urge to stand up and pull her into his arms made him hot all over. He had to get her out of here.

Clayton gave her a long, assessing look. "I keep wondering just what a pretty woman plans to do in a town like Crazy Creek. Why you'd go to bat for some man you don't know from Adam."

Irene opened her mouth, then closed it and

thought for a moment. She told herself she did it because she needed the experience.

"I have never handled a murder case before," she heard herself confess.

"Thought so," Clayton said, his voice quiet.

Her head came up. "We're going to win. I am a very capable attorney."

"Thought that, too," he responded. "Just curious is all."

"About what, exactly?" Her tone sounded extra prim, even to her.

"About you. And me."

Her pulse jumped. She should end this conversation. Now. Go back to her safe, protected home and…read or write a letter to Nora or do *something*. Anything. Even knit. The longer she listened to his voice, feeling her blood thrum in her ears, the more vulnerable she felt.

She was off balance around him. The tension building between herself and this man was almost unbearable. Her temples throbbed. She couldn't seem to catch her breath.

Against her better judgment, she gathered up the deck and reshuffled it with shaking hands. For want of anything better to do, she laid out five cards each.

His long fingers folded themselves around his cards, but he didn't look at them. "I haven't been doing much thinking beyond not dangling at the end of a rope.''

Irene heard his words through a jumble of her own thoughts. She could save him, she knew she could. Now that Judge Phipps would subpoena her two key witnesses, it was just a matter of getting them to corroborate her findings. The jury would surely acquit him.

And what then?

He will thank you and head for Texas.

A needle of pain laced across her chest. ''Well, you're not going to hang.''

His dark gray eyes regarded her with studied detachment. ''You think not?''

She nodded. ''I think not.'' Then she heard herself add, ''The question is, what will you do then?''

He hefted himself off the cot, slowly stood up, and stepped around the upturned barrel to grasp her elbow. ''That's enough talk for one evening. I'll escort you to the door.''

He lifted the key from the cracker barrel, reached outside and unlocked the cell.

''But we didn't finish—''

His fingers tightened on her arm. ''Yes, we did.''

He walked her past the sheriff, nodding over his paper-jumbled desk. As they passed the stove,

Clayton moved the coffeepot onto the heat. At the open doorway, he released her.

He stood so close she could hear his breathing. "Get on out of here, Irene."

She could not utter one single word. On unsteady legs she found her way down the street to the Maybud Hotel dining room, where she sat for an hour staring into a cup of cold black coffee, wondering what on earth she wanted from this man.

Chapter Twelve

Clayton watched his attorney make her way through the jostling courtroom crowd and settle herself beside him at the counsel table.

"Morning," he offered.

"Good morning, Mr. Black." Her voice was as crisp and businesslike as a new dollar bill.

He inclined his head toward her. "*Mr*. Black, is it? If I remember right," he said in a low voice, "I wallpapered your dining room, took you to dinner and taught you to play poker. Somewhere along the way I even kissed you good night. And—" his voice dropped to a whisper "—you're still calling me 'mister'?"

She fluffed the ruffle on the hem of her yellow dimity dress. "In this courtroom, Mr. Black, we are client and attorney. Across the poker table, we…you can be anything you like."

She refused to meet his eyes.

Last night she'd called him Clayton, not mister. He couldn't sleep after she left. The faint, sweet scent of lilac water wafted through his cell and he lay awake, thinking about all kinds of things— Texas. The ranch near Allenville. The sugar plantation in Louisiana that had belonged to his mother. Brance Fortier.

And his lawyer, Irene Hardisson.

Now it was ten o'clock and already too hot for the flies to even buzz against the window. The few women in the restless crowd fanned themselves with their aprons or a bunched-up page from the *Crazy Creek Reader.* One lady in a heavily veiled hat used a pleated paper fan. She whacked it back and forth with quick, jerky motions that just missed her chin. An unfinished piece of needlework spread over her lap—some kind of embroidery.

During earlier sessions, Clayton had watched her dart a long silver needle in and out of the cloth square while Irene questioned Doc Martin and the Cedarville undertaker under oath. He thought she'd pretty well proved his innocence until Lawyer Montgomery cross-examined.

The prosecuting attorney and Judge Phipps together had poked prairie wagon-size holes in their testimony. Irene had objected until her voice was hoarse. The dark-haired woman in the crowd bent her head and stabbed away at her needlework. There was something familiar about her, he thought, until he remembered she had been there, in the same chair, on the opening day of his trial.

After the lunch recess, even the men in the gallery began to fan themselves. Bandannas floated over faces flushed with heat. One man in a faded blue Union army shirt waved his hand back and forth in front of his face. Pages of the newspaper were divided up among ranchers and cowhands, the inked sheets folded, pleated and flapped awkwardly in the heavy, still air of the stifling courtroom.

Clayton sweltered in silence. Irene, he noticed, used her little ruffled silk fan only when deep in thought. Otherwise, it lay at her elbow on the counsel table while she scribbled notes.

He was sorely tempted to pick it up himself. Sweat from the back of his neck soaked his shirt collar. It didn't help matters much when Lawyer Montgomery recalled him to the witness box.

The prosecuting attorney paced before him, pumping his black top hat up and down to create a movement of air. Suddenly he stopped.

"Mr. Black, did you ever kill anyone?"

"I'm a Texas Ranger. It kinda goes with the territory."

"How did you do it?"

"Shot 'em, mostly. One time I had to knife an hombre I was taking in to Fort—"

"*Had* to? Did you say *had* to?"

"Hell, yes, I had to. He was wanted for robbing a train and he got the jump on me. It was him or me."

Irene was on her feet in an instant. "Objection!" she rasped. "Your Honor, this line of questioning diverges from—"

"Mighty interesting, though," Judge Phipps drawled. "Overruled."

Clayton watched her small white teeth clamp down on her lower lip. It was a gesture he'd grown to recognize, one she used when she was losing. Or exasperated. Any minute he expected the willowy young woman swathed in yellow pleats and gathers to explode.

She fisted both hands and plopped onto her chair as Lawyer Montgomery resumed his questioning.

"You ever plan to kill anyone *outside* the line of duty?"

Clayton's eyes sought Irene's. She'd warned him about admitting too much about the incident in New Orleans. Yet here was the question, and he was under oath to tell the truth. He'd sworn vengeance, one way or the other, on Brance Fortier.

She gazed back at him a long time, her expression agonized. Then, almost imperceptibly, her head tipped forward.

"Yep," Clayton replied. "I'm sorry to say that I have."

Lawyer Montgomery's eyes lit up. "Aha" he

exulted. Furiously he fanned his hat back and forth in the vicinity of his narrow face.

Judge Phipps leaned forward, his sharp, dark eyes riveted on Clayton.

"And just whom," enunciated the prosecuting attorney with an elaborate swish of his hat, "did you plot to kill?"

Clayton saw Irene's eyes close. Her lips moved in what he suspected was a silent prayer.

"It was..." He hesitated. "Someone who'd done injury to my family. Someone who deserved to die."

A collective gasp went up from the gallery, followed by a low droning noise, like angry bees. "Deserved to die?" someone shouted. "Didja hear what he said—he planned it!"

Clayton tried to locate the speaker, wanted to make eye contact with the person. Wanted to explain.

Lawyer Montgomery's thin lips widened into a feral grin. "Was this person someone you knew?"

"Objection!" Irene cried out over the growing tumult. "This matter is irrelevant. There is no connection between—"

Her sentence was obliterated by the pounding of the gavel. "Overruled! Answer the question, son."

"But Your Honor—"

"I said overruled, by damn." The judge nodded to Lawyer Montgomery. "Proceed."

"No!" Irene brought her small balled-up fist down onto the counsel table. "This is unconscionable!"

"Oh, my," the judge said. "I do like them four-bit words, little lady. But you let loose with one more, and I'm gonna find you in contempt. Now siddown and hush up! Repeat the question, Mr. Montgomery."

The prosecutor waited until the courtroom noise ebbed. "I repeat, was this unfortunate person—the one who 'deserved to die'—someone you knew?"

Clayton thought about refusing to answer. Then he'd be held in contempt, he supposed. Either way, he'd still be in jail. He caught Irene's gaze and held it. He couldn't see *her* going to jail as well; he might as well get it over with.

"The man was my uncle."

Pandemonium broke loose. "Murderer!" a woman screamed. *"Murderer!"*

The judge gaveled for order, to no avail. Suddenly Irene was on her feet, moving toward the bench. Judge Phipps leaned over while she spoke rapidly into his ear. He began nodding and gaveling at the same instant. Irene whirled away and came toward Clayton.

"Court's adjourned till tomorrow," the judge shouted. He signaled the bailiff. "Jase, tell 'em, will you?"

The bailiff squared his burly shoulders and

opened his mouth. "Court's adjourned," he bellowed.

Shouts of "No" stuttered back at him. "We want that murderin' SOB to pay fer what he done!"

"Let's try the bastard ourselves!"

"Let's hang him now and get it over with!"

A man leaped to his feet and pantomimed tossing a rope around Clayton's neck.

Irene grabbed the bailiff's shirt sleeve and yanked hard. "Quick! Take the prisoner back to the jail!"

The bailiff looked toward the bench. At a signal from the judge, he strode forward and wrestled Clayton through the maddened spectators to the door. The hulking man didn't have to muscle him too hard, Clayton acknowledged.

Judge Phipps whacked away with his gavel, but the crowd was clearly getting out of hand. Clayton couldn't get back to the safety of his jail cell fast enough.

The last thing he glimpsed before his cell door banged shut on the milling crowd was the dark-haired lady, calmly holding her embroidery. At the sight, a chill went down his spine.

Irene snatched the key to her client's jail cell from the hook and jammed it into the lock.

With his good arm Clayton pushed his hat off

his face and sat up on the cot. "What the—a little late for poker, isn't it?"

"Get up," she ordered. "And hurry."

"Now, why should—"

Irene pinned him with eyes that shot sparks. "There's a lynching party on its way over. Come with me."

Without another word, she grabbed the barrel they'd used as a poker table and dragged it over to the small window. "Can you fit through there?" she demanded.

He sized up the opening and nodded.

"Go, then. I'll be right behind you."

Clayton blinked. "You've got to be joking. You can't get all those layers of petticoats through that little space!"

A shout went up from the front of the building. Flickering red-gold torchlight danced off the adobe walls.

"Yes, I can!" she snapped. "Hurry!"

He set his foot on the barrel, anchored his knee on the adobe sill and grasped the upper window frame with his good arm. He propelled himself out feet first. Good thing they hadn't put bars on the window.

Behind him, Irene climbed onto the barrel and thrust her head and shoulders through the opening. She reached out her arms to him. "Pull," she whispered.

He grasped one wrist and drew her forward. Inch by inch, she wriggled through the window, her petticoats scrunching, her pantaletted knees scraping on the rough stone. Outside, Clayton caught her about the waist and helped her to stand.

A gunshot echoed from the street in front of the jail.

"Come on," he said. He pulled her into the shadow of the building and then stopped. Both of them were panting hard.

"I could steal a horse," he volunteered.

"They'd catch you and hang you on the spot. We have to get to my house."

"Are you kidding?"

Another gunshot.

"No. And *they're* not, either. Come on!"

They snaked in and out of back alleys and shadows until the serene-looking white house came into view.

"My bedroom is on the second floor—the one with the lace curtains," she whispered.

"I'll get to the roof. Prop the window open."

She nodded and turned away. Switching her skirt into place, she batted at the dust, and as she marched toward Park Street, she heard his low chuckle.

Head erect, looking straight ahead, Irene mounted the porch steps and opened the front door. She resisted the temptation to scamper as fast as

she could up the stairway. Instead, she ascended
the polished wood treads in as slow and ladylike a
manner as possible.

But beneath her bodice, her heart pounded like
a sledgehammer.

What I wouldn't give for wings, Clayton thought
as he jockeyed his torso onto the low porch over-
hang. *Or two good arms.* His shoulder wound
throbbed with the effort of levering his body
weight up and over the roof edge. Ahead of him,
the glow of a kerosene lamp illuminated a square
of white lace.

He made slow, quiet progress toward it, then
heard the scrape of the sash being raised. The lamp
dimmed and went out.

Good girl. Otherwise, he'd be silhouetted in the
window frame.

He dropped noiselessly through the opening and
stood up. ''Irene?'' he whispered.

''Over here. By the door.''

He waited until his eyes adjusted to the dark,
then scanned the room. The sparse furnishings
made bulky shadows along the walls. As his gaze
moved from shape to shape, a glimmer of something light colored caught his attention.

In the silence he could hear her breathing.

She didn't move as he stepped toward her.

"I bolted the door," she said, keeping her voice low.

Clayton smiled. This was a woman who thought ahead.

"Come away from it," he instructed. "If they come looking, a bullet might catch you in the butt."

"Mr. Black, really!" But she glided to one side, positioning herself between two dark structures he took to be bureaus set against the far wall. "Surely they wouldn't dare enter my home!"

"I wouldn't bet on it."

"What do we do now?" she whispered.

"Wait."

"For how long?"

"As long as it takes. They'll search the town. If they don't find me, they'll figure I've lit out."

"*If*," she reiterated. "What if they *do* find you?"

Clayton grinned in the dark. "Well, then, Miss Hardisson, my guess is you'll be pretty well compromised. Most people flap their tongues over a man caught in a lady's bedroom."

Her sharp intake of breath told him she hadn't considered the risk to her reputation when she'd rescued him. Just as well. If she'd thought it all out, she'd have probably left him in jail.

"Oh," she said in a small voice. And then "oh" again, more softly.

"You might want to sit down. Could be a long night."

"What? Oh, yes. Of course." He heard the rustle of petticoats, then the creak of bedsprings. He stationed himself on one side of the open window where he could see the street below.

An hour crept by during which neither of them moved. Clayton heard shouting and the thud of horses' hooves near the jail, but so far no torchlight brands moved their way.

"Must be pretty liquored up if they haven't figured it out by now. Maybe they'll give up and go home to sleep it off."

He yawned and shifted his weight to his other foot. He'd give anything to have his rifle with him. He didn't like being a sitting duck.

"Best get some rest."

"I am resting," came her low reply. "At least my eyes are resting. However, my heart is beating like a tom-tom."

"Mine, too," he admitted.

He watched the patch of pale material he knew to be her full skirt shift position. Little by little the upper part of her torso tipped sideways until a final rustle and a soft sigh told him she had fallen asleep.

Clayton felt an overpowering urge to cover her with something, a quilt or a shawl. Finally he settled on the flounced edge of the counterpane. Tiptoeing to the bed, he pulled the soft material around her arms and shoulders. His hand shook.

She mumbled something and curled her knees into her chest.

He pulled a chair to the window, settled one knee against the sill. Another hour passed. For a time he imagined he was keeping watch over her instead of peeling his eyes for trouble in the street below. The thought made him feel warm all over.

When the pounding began, Clayton jerked to attention. The front door would splinter if they kept it up. He thought about easing noiselessly out the window, but then reasoned the roof outside would be the first place they'd look. The smartest move would be to position himself where they *wouldn't* be likely to look.

But where? The tall wardrobe, maybe. No, too obvious. Under the bed? Again, too obvious.

"Miss Hardisson, you up there?" a raucous voice shouted from downstairs. "We're comin' up!"

A sucked-in gasp of air and a glimmery movement on the bed told him the ruckus had wakened her.

"Yes," she called out. "What is it?"

"Open the door, ma'am. It's Sheriff Calder."

Clayton moved quickly to her bedside. "Stall 'em," he ordered, keeping his voice low.

"All right," she whispered. "I'll do my best."

"Ma'am?" the voice outside the door bellowed.

"Just a moment, Sheriff, while I...light a lamp," she finished hurriedly.

Clayton nodded in satisfaction. She sure could think on her feet.

"And," she continued in a quavery voice, "let me don a night robe. I was asleep, you see, and—"

"All right, ma'am. But hurry it up!"

"Oh heavens," she whispered. "I'll have to un..." Her sentence trailed off.

In the next instant Clayton heard a button snap off. It hit the floor with a little ping and suddenly he realized what she was doing—removing her dress! A swishing sound told him the rest of the story, and then two circles of pale material dotted the floor. She was shedding her petticoats.

The banging on the door resumed as another white cloud floated to the floor. "Miss Hardisson?"

"Quick," she whispered. "In the top drawer. My night robe."

Instantly he glided to the bureau and slid open the drawer. He drew out the first thing he touched, a silky soft garment of some kind, and tossed it toward the slender figure in the shadows.

"Matches," she hissed. "On the dresser."

Right. He waited until she had had time to draw on the night robe and then raked his thumbnail across the sulfur match head. Just as the lamplight flared, he saw her kick her black leather shoes under the bed.

Barefoot, she advanced toward him, her arm outstretched. He placed the lantern in her hand.

"Miss Hardisson, open up!"

For a split second, she gazed at him. Her eyes were huge. Her teeth worked at her lower lip, but she managed a shaky smile. Clayton's heart melted into a puddle of warm butter.

"I'm comin' in," the sheriff yelled.

She turned white. Silently she pointed to the wall next to the door, and he stepped into place. When the door swung open, he would be concealed from view.

"Give me a moment to unbolt the door, Sheriff. I was fast asleep." With quick, jerky motions she pulled the hairpins from the prim, upswept bun atop her head. Dark waves of shining hair tumbled to her shoulders.

Clayton sucked in his breath as she grappled with the metal bolt. With one final, agonized glance into his eyes, she released the catch and the door swung inward.

"Why, good evening, Sheriff Calder. I had retired and did not hear your knock."

"Evenin', ma'am." The pudgy lawman stepped onto the threshold, pushing the door farther open. Clayton pressed his shoulders against the wall.

''May I ask what is so important that you would disturb me at this hour of the night?'' Her voice sounded calm enough. He could see only a small portion of her right shoulder, but the rose-colored material of her robe fluttered like breeze-blown aspen leaves.

''Well, Miss Hardisson, there's been a jail-break.'' He spoke over the babble of raised male voices from the hallway. ''That murderin' Ranger fella got away somehow, and—quiet out there, Jase! I can't hear myself think! Anyway, ma'am I thought seein' as how you're his lawyer and all, he, uh, mighta come to you.''

''It is true I am Mr. Black's attorney, Sheriff Calder. However, I am certainly not his keeper. Where has Mr. Black gone?''

The sheriff edged a step farther into the room. ''You seen anything unusual tonight, ma'am?''

Clayton heard Irene draw in a long breath. ''Why yes, Sheriff. As a matter of fact I have.''

His entire body tensed.

''A mouse invaded my room earlier this evening. I hurried through my toilette—in fact, I unrobed myself in unseemly haste, as you can see—'' she gestured around the room with the lamp ''—and immediately retired to my bed.''

The sheriff ahemmed. Clayton pictured his slightly bulging eyes scanning the room, seeing the dress and the petticoats, three soft puddles of white muslin, like floppy flower heads sprouting from the plank floor.

"I am quite terrified of mice," she added.

Behind the door, Clayton suppressed a chuckle. At her next words, his grin broadened.

"Sheriff Calder, I wonder if I might beg your aid?"

"Ma'am?"

"Would…would you check under my bed? I thought I heard something scratching a while ago."

'Uh…oh, sure. Shut up out there, Jase! Sure, Miss Hardisson, I'll take a look."

The thud of boots and then a softer bump—the sheriff's knees hitting the floor—told Clayton everything. The sheriff was peering under the bed.

"Nuthin' under there 'cept shoes, ma'am. You want me to fish 'em out?"

"If you please, Sheriff. I would be most grateful."

Another thump. "There y'are, ma'am. By the way, I notice yer window's wide-open."

"Yes," Irene responded. "I always sleep with the sash up. My father back in Philadelphia advised plenty of fresh air."

"Might be wise to keep it closed tonight. You don't want that Black feller crawlin' in to hold you hostage."

"Oh! Why, that would be perfectly dreadful! Surely you don't think he would?"

"Nah. I think our murderer's hightailed it outta here. Jase, for the last time, pipe down out there! Prob'ly headin' south to Texas right this minute."

"I'm sure you're right, Sheriff. What a relief to know nothing—neither mouse nor man—will further disturb my rest. I cannot thank you enough."

The sheriff's knees cracked as he got to his feet. "T'ain't nuthin', ma'am. Jase!" He bellowed over his shoulder. "You men check the alley behind the house."

He backed out, tipping his hat. "Sorry t'trouble you, Miss Hardisson. An' don't bother your pretty head 'bout Mr. Clayton Black no more. Good riddance is what I say."

"Oh, yes, I'm sure," she agreed. "Good riddance, indeed."

"I'm comin' out, Jase! Don't shoot me! Damned trigger-happy posse," he muttered. The sheriff banged the door shut after him. From the other side his raspy voice rose in a final admonition. "Keep yer door locked and bolted, ma'am."

His footsteps thumped off down the hallway, and in a few seconds an echoing chorus of boots clattered down the stairs. There must have been ten men in the posse, Clayton figured from the sounds he heard through the door. If they'd found him, he wouldn't have stood a chance. He owed his life to lawyer Irene Hardisson.

They stared at each other for a long moment in silence. Her eyes were a fathomless green, dilated so hugely they looked like mossy pools.

"Did I do all right?" she whispered.

"Yeah." He grinned at her. "All except the 'good riddance' part."

"Well of course I didn't mean—"

Clayton stepped away from the wall and slipped the bolt home. "Miss Hardisson, you are a very handy lady to have around at a time like this. I especially admired the part about the mouse."

"Oh, well, I—I'm told I have a knack for acting. Papa abhorred the thought of my going on the stage, however. Perhaps that is why he took such pains with my law training. No respectable lady disports herself in a public place."

"Unless it's a courtroom," Clayton observed.

"Yes." She blushed. "Papa would die if—" She stopped short and pressed her hand to her mouth. Tears shone in her eyes.

"Your father is dead, isn't he?" Clayton inquired, his tone gentle.

She nodded and turned away. "I'll just pick up my petticoats," she said in a strangled voice.

"I think he'd be proud of what you did tonight."

She pivoted toward him, a lace-edged undergarment in her hands. "Do you really think so? About the mouse and everything? It was a lie, of course, and I hate to prevaricate, but—"

Clayton stepped toward her. "I really think so. And I also think we should douse the lamp, pronto!" He bent over the glass chimney, turned down the wick and puffed out the flame.

"Now what?" she whispered.

Good question, he thought. The picture of Irene Hardisson, her wavy dark hair tumbling loose about her shoulders, the silky rose night robe clutched about her slim body, burned in his memory. Her scent, the subtle spicy-sweet fragrance that wafted from her clothes, her person, made his body ache with longing. She was so *female.*

He remembered a moonlit night in the mountains of Colorado when a wolf's howl for its mate brought him to his knees. God in heaven, he, too, was hungry—hungry in body and even more in soul. But unlike the wolf, he didn't need just coupling, which was easily obtained, but spiritual connection, which was not.

And here she was, standing before him half-clothed. Desirable. And trusting.

He turned away.

"Now what?" she repeated.

"Now," he said in a voice gone suddenly hoarse, "we need to get some sleep."

"Oh. Of course."

"You take the bed. I'll settle down on the floor."

She did not answer, simply moved away from him. He heard the swish of the counterpane and then a soft plop at his feet. A pillow. The coverlet followed.

"Much obliged," he murmured.

"Good night, Mr. Black."

"Good night, Miss Hardisson."

Clayton lay down beneath the open window, positioned the pillow under his head, and with his good arm pulled the bedcover over his body.

"Good night." He waited five full heartbeats, then added a single word in a voice he was sure she could not hear. "Irene."

He rolled her name over and over on his tongue and felt the hot pull of desire in his groin.

Chapter Thirteen

Irene lay unmoving in the big double bed, her body curled into a ball, knees to chin. She could not stop her trembling, although she worked hard to calm her ragged breathing. What if she had not succeeded in distracting Sheriff Calder with the imaginary mouse? What if he had glimpsed Clayton behind the door?

Think logically! she commanded herself. If Clayton *had* been discovered in her room, the bunch of hotheads led by the bumbling sheriff would have lynched him. She'd heard of such travesties of justice in the West. Out here in this untamed, lawless wilderness the rules of the civilized world were often ignored in favor of expediency.

She hated to admit it, but Philadelphia had left its indelible stamp on her sensibilities. She preferred law and order, refined manners, and cream in her coffee.

And yet, life in a big Eastern city was a bit...well, boring. She liked the vitality of the West, the sense of adventure and independence.

She even liked the people. Clayton Black, for one.

But she did *not* like being scared out of her wits by a sheriff and his posse at two o'clock in the morning!

A nagging unease worked on her conscience. What a scandalous thing she had done, breaking a man—an accused criminal—out of jail and harboring him in her bedroom.

On the other hand, the alternative, a lynching, was equally beyond the pale. She simply did what she had to do, what any person with a shred of decency would be compelled to do. Her father would approve. Judge Phipps himself would approve. He might be cantankerous and prejudiced in favor of the prosecution, but at bottom the judge knew right from wrong. She knew he would want her to protect her client.

Her breathing stopped altogether at the thought of the tall, intriguing man asleep on her bedroom floor. Then the image of the sheriff, down on his hands and knees hunting her ''mouse,'' made her smile. A puzzling creature, the human male. Part manly bluster and pride and part pussycat.

She sobered in an instant. What would she— they—do, come morning? Did Clayton have some sort of escape plan? How could he get away without being seen?

She gave a little groan as she rolled over and curled up on her other side. She could not possibly sleep still trussed up in her whalebone corset. She hadn't had time to unlace it; in fact, she still had on her camisole and underdrawers. Even though it was hours after midnight, the air was still warm and breezeless. It was impossible to sleep under all these layers.

The corset stays dug into her waist. Silent as a shadow, she sat up and folded back the sheet. At least she could shed the night robe. Goodness knows, she didn't need that on top of everything else. She slipped out of it and tossed it onto the end of the bed, then loosened her lacings. Sinking back onto her pillow, she considered her situation.

Clayton would probably leave before dawn. He'd have to steal a horse, she supposed. He couldn't very well take the stagecoach—the whole town would recognize him the minute he set foot outside.

She flopped over on her other side. The sporadic scrape of crickets and the occasional soft hoofbeat of a horse floated through the open window. She lay still and listened to the slow, regular breathing of the man she had helped to escape.

In one way, she hated to see him leave. Clayton Black was the most interesting man she'd ever chanced on. He didn't talk much about himself, but she was an expert at gleaning bits of information. He had some knowledge of Dickens and Fenimore Cooper's works; he had never traveled abroad; no doubt he had never heard music other than a fiddle or a harmonica, had never admired a fine painting.

But even half-educated as he was, she liked talking with him. He knew different things, things not taught in colleges but learned through living. He understood people, held high standards of horse-flesh, believed in eye-for-an-eye justice and the subtle art of poker playing. And he was a gentle but exacting teacher.

One thing she knew beyond all doubt—she had certainly never met a man like him.

And you have no reason in the world to think of him any longer. Tomorrow morning he would head south.

Besides, while she might admire the man, their backgrounds were so different a lasting connection was out of the question. He preferred days on horseback and nights playing poker; she preferred days in courtrooms and nights poring over law-books.

What a pity… she thought drowsily. *We might have become great friends.*

She yawned, pulled the muslin sheet up to her now-bare shoulders, and her thoughts drifted off.

* * *

Clayton stood it on the hard plank floor as long as he could. When the throbbing in his wounded shoulder got so bad he couldn't sleep, he sat up and surveyed the bed. There was a lot of mattress, and not very much of her. Maybe he could...

He didn't even finish the thought before he was on his feet. Quiet as a cat, he eased his weight onto the far side of the bed. When he lay full length, his boots touched the footboard.

With his good arm, he stuffed the pillow he'd carried with him under his head, closed his eyes and breathed a sigh of relief. Definitely better. With any luck at all, she wouldn't wake up until he'd got at least an hour's worth of shut-eye. He couldn't ride very far without it.

He folded his hands across his belt buckle and rolled to take the weight off his shoulder. His bent knees just touched the mound of quilt that must be her bottom.

A hot shiver went through him at the thought. All that separated them was a single layer of bed-clothes.

And about a thousand and one other things. Like background and breeding and...oh, what the hell. No lily-white lawyer from an Eastern city would look twice at a half French, half Cherokee ranch-bred Texan who couldn't spell half the words she used.

She was sure all woman, though. Her body

warmth, its subtle, sweet fragrance, stirred him as no other woman's ever had. And that spelled danger.

Never again could he allow himself to care about another human being, especially not a woman. Losing someone you loved hurt too much.

Because of the life he'd chosen for himself, he couldn't risk being close to anyone. A Texas Ranger was a tough but lonely breed, he acknowledged. He'd known that when he'd joined up; that was part of the bargain.

"A woman'll tie your heart up so you can't shoot straight," his father had told him.

He would never, ever, risk that again.

So, Lawyer Hardisson, it's tonight for us, and I hope you don't mind me sleepin' by your side like this, but the honest-to-God truth is I'm lonely as hell and a little taste of a woman like you is all I'm ever gonna get.

He folded his body around the soft lump her form made under the sheet and gently laid his arm over her. She smelled good. Sweet and fresh and so tantalizing it made his groin ache.

In the morning, he promised himself, he'd set about doing what he had to do. In the meantime, he'd close his eyes and pretend he belonged here, by her side.

Irene woke only once and felt something warm pressing at her back. Without looking, she knew it was Clayton.

Part of her was shocked. Horrified! The man had actually invited himself into—well, onto—her bed! Another part of her wanted to scoot backward against his solid, comforting body and dream away the rest of the night.

As she pondered what she should do, her lids grew heavier and heavier.

When she awoke at dawn, he was gone.

Feeling oddly bereft, she struggled to her feet and splashed lukewarm water from the washbasin on her face and neck. Her body felt as heavy as her travel trunk. She had no interest in a proper toilette, and drew on the first dress she found when she opened the wardrobe—a pale rose check gingham. Completely unsuitable for a courtroom appearance, but since there wouldn't be any more trial, it wouldn't matter. She would seek out Judge Phipps and explain everything.

She felt no enthusiasm for any of it. Not even the thought of hot coffee and fresh-baked biscuits and jam perked her spirits. She couldn't believe Clayton had left for Texas without a single word of farewell—a note, anything. Men like Clayton Black were like that, she supposed. Rolling stones.

With uninspired motions, she brushed out her hair and wound it into the French twist Papa had favored. Then she dragged herself down the stairs and over to the Maybud Hotel dining room.

At the corner table, casually perusing the *Crazy Creek Reader,* sat Clayton Black, of all people. He rose at the sight of her and gallantly tipped his hat. "Miss Hardisson."

"What on earth are you doing here?" Irene demanded.

"Eating my breakfast," he replied, his tone matter-of-fact. "Care to join me?"

"No! Yes!" She plopped onto the chair he pulled out and stared at him for a full minute while he folded the newspaper and set it aside. Fury and elation warred in her brain.

How dare he show himself! Didn't he realize he would be recognized, arrested—even hung—by the same irate, drunken rowdies that hunted him last night? Why would he throw away the freedom she'd worked so hard—lied, even!—to gain for him?

"You are a low-down, ungrateful—"

"I had a talk with Judge Phipps this morning."

"—shortsighted, self-impor—what? *Judge Phipps?*"

Clayton nodded. "Phipps agrees the jail isn't secure. I explained everything to him. Didn't take much palaver, really—he said he worried all night about a lynching party. Feared it'd tarnish his reputation. Consequently—" he flagged the lone waitress and indicated a second cup for coffee ''—he's released me into your custody.''

''Custody! I thought you were leav—''

''Nope.''

''You're not heading for Texas?''

''Nope.''

Irene sat back, openmouthed, as the waitress brought a cup and filled it. ''You orderin' what the gentleman's havin'?''

''What? Oh, yes. Bring me the same.''

''If you say so, ma'am.''

''And some cream,'' Clayton added. ''For the lady.''

Irene waited until the aproned woman withdrew. ''Just what am I expected to *do* with your 'custody'?''

''Just the usual. Protect me. Make sure I don't leave town.''

Irene met his amused expression with a frown. ''Why did you not leave? Surely you had the chance?''

Clayton tapped his head with his forefinger. ''Think, Miss Hardisson. What kind of reputation would I have if I skipped out on a murder charge? A Texas Ranger would put an end to his career that way.''

''Oh. I see.'' She didn't, really. She thought surely he would have grabbed the opportunity to escape.

"Phipps and the sheriff think the townsfolk aren't so riled up today," he continued, stirring another spoonful of sugar into his coffee. "Most of the men have pretty big headaches this morning. So I told 'em I'd be in court this morning at ten, like always, so the trial can go on."

Irene gazed at him, uncomprehending.

"I have to get a judgment before I go back to Texas," he explained. "For my own peace of mind, if nothing else."

"You went to the sheriff?"

Clayton sent her an engaging smile. "Sure as hell did. He 'bout choked on his ceegar, but after a while he saw my side of it."

"Oh, my gracious me," Irene breathed. "You are either a complete fool or a man of great courage."

"Think so?"

"Yes. I do."

Clayton chuckled. "Wait till you see the breakfast you ordered."

It arrived at that moment. A seven-high stack of flapjacks, four fried eggs, and a steak.

Irene blanched. "I can't eat all this!"

"Don't worry about it," Clayton said, slicing into his meat. "After a week on jailhouse grub, I'll finish what you don't put away."

Irene picked up her fork. Despite the joy that bubbled up inside at seeing him this morning, her elation at realizing he had not left town without saying goodbye, she clenched her jaw in exasperation at his cool, collected manner under the circumstances.

Voluntarily staying in Crazy Creek for the trial? It was dangerous. The townspeople were misinformed and angry, Judge Phipps was clearly one-sided, and her opponent, Lawyer Montgomery, at first appeared inept but in actuality was crafty as a hungry fox.

This whole thing was turning into a circus.

Therefore, she reasoned, jabbing systematically at the four egg yolks on the plate before her, *the situation calls for extraordinary measures.*

She attacked the pancakes with the same studied determination, a plan already forming in her mind.

Chapter Fourteen

A subdued crowd of spectators jammed the Crazy Creek courtroom. Before the bailiff could bellow "All rise," Judge Phipps appeared and strode to his seat behind the bench. The old man shook the gavel as he spoke.

"This here's a law-abidin' court. Any more outbursts like we had yesterday and I'll throw the whole lot of you in jail for disturbing the peace! Is that understood?"

Heads nodded. No one dared even clear a throat or blow a nose, Clayton noted. The heavy silence pressed at his back. To his left, the seven men of the jury sat loosening their collars or staring at their boots. He noted that the dark-haired woman with the embroidery frame sat straight as a rifle barrel, stabbing her needle up and down.

The gavel crashed, and one elderly farmer let

out a squeak of surprise. A ripple of laughter rolled around the courtroom.

"Order in the court!" Judge Phipps yelled, and silence again descended. Lawyer Montgomery's watery gaze swept over the jury, then studied Clayton where he sat at the counsel table. A tiny smile curved the attorney's thin lips.

All through yesterday's testimony by Dr. Martin and undertaker Seamus Moody, the prosecutor had stared at Clayton with the smug, satisfied look of an overfed cat.

"Prosecution may proceed," the judge intoned.

Lawyer Montgomery rose and gazed out the window for a long moment. "Your Honor, it is my view that the testimony of Dr. Martin and Mr. Moody, which we heard yesterday morning, regarding the bullets removed from the chest of the deceased and the shoulder of the defendant, proves nothing of any consequence. It's the hand that pointed the gun—nay, the finger that pulled the trigger we need to establish."

Irene leaped to her feet. "My client is innocent! The proof is in those bullets I presented the second day of this proceeding." She advanced toward the jury. "You remember, Mr. Marsh. You were the one who correctly identified the—"

"Objection!" Lawyer Montgomery waved his long, skinny arm at the judge. "I don't recall that she proved—"

"Sustained."

Irene whirled toward her opponent. "Mr. Montgomery, your lapse of memory is most unprofessional. Why, even Mr. Marsh, here, remembers the incontrovertible evidence I introduced. Are you, sir, so certain of your mental faculties that you could swear you did not see what every other person in this courtroom *did* see?"

"Well, sure I am. I mean, I saw it and all, but—"

"Ah, now, Mr. Montgomery. Now you say you *did* see it. Which is it, sir?"

Montgomery swallowed audibly. "What I mean is—"

Irene held up one hand. "One moment. Allow me to conduct a small experiment." She stepped toward him. "Face me, if you please. Outside that window—no, do not look!—is a hitching rail." She glanced over the prosecutor's shoulder. "There is one horse tied to it."

"Yes, I remember seeing it when I came in."

"There was something unusual about that horse, was there not?"

"Unusual? Well, now I recollect it had an old beat-up straw hat between its ears, if that's what you mean."

Irene's eyebrows shot up. "An *old, beat-up straw hat*? Mr. Montgomery, are you sure of that? Don't peek, now—just rely on your memory."

Clayton noticed Judge Phipps peering out the window.

Montgomery sniffed. "Course I'm sure. It isn't that often you see a horse with a straw hat on."

The heads of the jury members swiveled in unison toward the window. Some of the men began to grin.

"Are you absolutely positive about that 'old, beat-up straw hat'?" Irene pursued.

"Yes indeed, I am absolutely positive!" Lawyer Montgomery's voice rose with each word uttered. "Positive" boomed out in a shout.

Irene smiled at him. "Positive," she murmured. She shook her head. "I offer my deepest sympathy on your affliction, Mr. Montgomery. I am just grateful none of these sharp-eyed, levelheaded members of the jury are thus hampered."

Lawyer Montgomery spun toward the window and squinted his eyes. Mouth gaping, he snatched off his spectacles and craned his neck for a better view.

Clayton followed his gaze. Outside the courtroom there was indeed a single mare tied to the rail. And on its head perched a hat, sure enough. But what was now convulsing the spectators and causing Lawyer Montgomery to goggle as if he had apoplexy was the hat. It was Irene Hardisson's spectacular-looking creation with the bright red cherries on top.

"Haw, haw, haw," the bailiff chortled. Even the judge chuckled.

"All right, little lady, you proved your point. Montgomery?" He directed a stern look at the prosecuting attorney. "You pay attention, you hear?"

His pale eyes bulging in disbelief, Montgomery nodded and sank into his chair amid the snickers circulating among the onlookers. All seemed to enjoy the joke, except for the embroidery lady, who bent her veiled head over her wooden frame in studious concentration.

Irene seized her advantage. "One little misperception is not so grave a sin. But a man's life is at stake—an innocent man, as Dr. Martin and Mr. Moody and I have demonstrated. Some of you acutely observant men and women must acknowledge that fact."

The spectators glanced at their neighbors and straightened in their seats. One woman poked her husband with her elbow. "I seen it right off," she said in an audible whisper. "That hat—nobody could miss that hat! Nor them bullets she showed us, neither!"

"Order!" The judge's gavel banged down. "Get on with it."

Irene sent him a dazzling smile. "Judge Phipps, in accordance with our arrangement..." She paused and glanced at Clayton.

"Objection!" Lawyer Montgomery was on his feet again. "You must understand that I know nothing of an 'arrangement.'"

"Oh, of course, Mr. Montgomery," Irene purred. "It is fully understood that you know nothing whatsoever."

"Thank you." The prosecuting attorney said over the guffaws erupting around him. "I mean…uh, well that is, I—"

Clayton had to hand it to her—in ten minutes she'd completely destroyed the man's credibility.

Montgomery exploded. "Your Honor, this—what Miz Hardisson's doing—well, it's downright unconstitutional!"

"Don't preach the law to me, son. I know what's constitutional."

"But—"

The judge warmed to his subject. "Well now, the Constitution's a bit like an unmarried woman. It's got to be—excuse my language, Miss Hardisson—violated some to reach its full flower."

Clayton saw Irene wince and bite her lower lip. He could guess what her ploy had cost her in the way of ethical ideals. Now he wondered what she'd do in the face of the judge's tasteless analogy. Even if the unconstitutionality worked to his and Irene's advantage, he knew no straight-arrow lawyer who preferred walking the high road could stomach too much illegality.

"You are quite right, I'm sure, Your Honor," she responded.

Astounded, Clayton stared at the diminutive figure in ruffled rose gingham. She looked as delicate and appealing as a wild rose, yet here she stood, sparring with Judge Phipps. How many more layers of this surprising woman might he discover?

He squelched the thought the instant it registered. He wasn't going to find out. He was going back to Texas, back to ranging. Back to his solitary life at the Double B ranch Pa had left him.

Hold up a damn minute, he reminded himself. He wasn't exactly free as a bird yet—he was on trial for his life. Could be he wouldn't *get* home to Texas.

A week ago, before Irene turned up in his jail cell, he didn't much care whether he lived or died. The verdict on his guilt or innocence didn't matter to him. Someone had done what he'd set out to do—taken revenge on Brance Fortier for the murder of his father and his sister. A week ago, his life hadn't mattered all that much to him. He'd have been glad to pay with his life if he had to.

Now, after a mere eight days in Irene's presence, admiring her intelligence and courage, laughing at her childlike excitement over a hand of poker, Clayton found he wanted desperately to live. Irene Hardisson, with her prim gait and her quick, intelligent eyes, and—Lordy, how could he forget?—

a round of poker later? Now that you've arranged for custody, you're stayin' at the hotel.''

"I am?" His words barely registered. *"I am?"*

"Second floor. Room next to mine, so you can keep an eye on me, like the judge said."

"Mr. Black...Clayton...there is no need for me—"

He grinned down at her. "That's what you think."

"Why? What are you planning?"

"Nothin' you'd care to hear about until the verdict's in." With his good arm he picked up her leather satchel and touched her elbow. "Come on. I'll make 'custody' easy. I'll walk you to the hotel."

Speechless, she stared at him. A part of her wanted to insist on *her* plan; another part of her liked being taken care of. Unconsciously she stepped along with him. His tall frame moved beside her, one long step to her two shorter ones. Her full gingham skirt brushed against his legs. When she drew it to one side, he spoke a single word. "Don't."

Her hand fell away. Irene caught her breath. The thought of being in the room next to his, all night, made her head buzz. Of course, she reasoned, it would be out of the question for him to stay at *her* house, unchaperoned. This way she understood he was doing what he could to protect her reputation.

They stepped off the boardwalk in unison, moved into the dusty street. Late afternoon sun blinded them. As they approached the opposite walkway, a skinny, towheaded youngster in faded overalls popped up from beside the hitching rail.

"Here's yer hat, miss. I throwed that old straw one away, just like you told me."

Irene fished a two-bit piece from her skirt pocket and plopped it into his grimy palm.

"Gee, thanks, ma'am!" He scampered away toward Bowman's mercantile.

"An accomplice?" Clayton queried in an amused tone.

Irene flicked a glance upward. "Let's just say a friend of the court."

His low laughter brought heat to her cheeks. She'd never before resorted to subterfuge during a trial. Out here in Crazy Creek the court proceedings were so topsy-turvy she was emboldened to tamp down her conscience and try anything short of outright perjury. To her surprise she was only mildly apologetic for this breach of protocol. It was worth every strategem she could come up with if it gained the unusual man striding beside her his freedom.

"I'm kinda at a loss how to entertain a lady

who's got me in custody,'' Clayton remarked. ''Any ideas?''

''A game of poker would be lovely,'' she said as they ascended the wide wooden steps to the Maybud Hotel lobby. ''But first I want a bath and some supper. Shall we say around eight o'clock?''

''Agreed.''

She headed for the desk clerk and her room key.

''Just one more question,'' he said at her back, keeping his voice low.

Irene spun toward him. ''And that is?''

''Your room, or mine?''

Irene's heart jumped violently under the rose gingham. She couldn't answer, couldn't utter a single word.

She clutched the key in her fist and pivoted toward the stairs.

Clayton followed her up. At her door, he closed her fingers around the handle of her satchel and stepped back. ''You decide.''

He unlocked her door and gently propelled her inside. Only when the latch clicked behind her did she recover her tongue.

''A lady never visits a gentleman's quarters,'' she announced to the door.

''So I've heard, ma'am,'' came the reply from the other side.

Irene took a deep breath. ''Well?''

"Well, what?" He sounded faintly amused. Good gracious sakes, would he force her to say it out loud? The very idea brought heat flooding into her chest.

Be honest with yourself, Irene. She longed for the diversion of a poker game. With him. She was a bundle of nerves after today's courtroom antics; she needed to do something to occupy her mind, to keep from pacing the floor all night working out the tension that knotted the muscles of her stomach. Playing poker with Clayton Black was always interesting. Besides, it was the only thing she could think of.

At this moment, outside of a bath and some supper, the only thing she wanted was to pit her intelligence against the puzzling man who tugged at her senses. Never in her life had she been so distracted by a male.

The realization left her insides quivery. Her powers of analysis told her it was more than boredom that made the prospect of betting against Clayton exciting. It was something else altogether.

"My room," she said in a pinched tone. "And I want to play for truths," she heard herself state.

"If you say so," he replied, his voice already fading. The thunk of a closing door cut off his low, rich laughter.

An hour later, after a thick steak and four cups of the Maybud Hotel's best coffee, the last cup served up with a shot of whiskey and carried to Irene's room on a tray, Clayton felt a good deal more relaxed.

It had been a long, crazy-quilt kind of a day. He was only too glad to put it behind him and concentrate on something other than trying to figure out Judge Phipps's interpretation of a fair trial and what made Prosecutor Montgomery tick. He was more interested in what went on in his inventive, observant lawyer's pretty head.

That surprised the hell out of him. Never in his entire experience with women—and he'd had his share—had he cared a single chicken feather about what went on in a lady's mind. In fact, the prettier the woman, the less he even noticed her brain.

Until now. Watching Irene Hardisson's moss-green eyes study the cards clutched in her slim, manicured fingers, he owned up to something. It didn't much matter what she looked like—how softly ruffled her dress, how her breasts pressed against the fabric when she inhaled.

He didn't care near as much about what she had on underneath as what she was thinking. Each time her dark eyebrows drew into a frown of concentration, when she nibbled her lower lip, lowered her lashes to hide the assessing expression in her gaze as she studied her cards, Clayton found himself biting his tongue.

What? he wanted to say. *Tell me what's going on inside you.*

He settled into the straight-back oak chair and recalculated the odds on the five cards he held in his hand. One good way to find out what she was thinking would be to win this first round. And if he did, as he expected to with two jacks and two fours fanned under his fingertips, why then it'd be easy. Just ask her.

One good thing about playing for truths—the game usually turned out to be more interesting than one expected. For starters, his first question would be—

"I bet two questions." She snapped her cards into a stack facedown on the side table they had drawn up between them and covered them with her palm.

"Two! Lady, that's a pretty bold bet! You want to reconsider?"

A secret light danced in her eyes. "No, thank you."

He decided to go for the full house. "I'll take one card."

He shuttered his glance as he looked at his draw. Maybe he could bluff her into folding.

"Raise or call."

She spread three sevens before him—sevens and fours. Low, but enough. He hadn't drawn the cards he needed. He'd have to fold. And lose.

She clapped her hands in delight, like a child exulting over a new toy, and Clayton groaned. He was the toy. By the rules of the game, she could now ferret out his innermost secrets. He was beginning to regret having taught her so well.

Irene pursed her lips, thinking. ''Very well, here is my first question. What do you want more than anything in the world?''

Freedom was the first thing that popped into his mind. No, wait. He'd rather have Pa and Jannie back, alive and happy as they had been before Fortier and the Cortina gang had turned up.

No, he didn't even want to consider the impossible—it was too painful. Money, then? Or whiskey? Springtime on the ranch and his old life with the Rangers?

''The truth, now,'' she reminded him.

''I'd like to spend the night in your bed,'' he blurted. *God Almighty, where had* that *sprung from?*

Her eyes widened, the pupils darkening gradually as his blunt statement sank in. Her lips opened. ''Is that—I mean, are you…um…that is, Mr. Black…that is your answer?''

Clayton closed his eyes at his own audacity. "I guess it is, since it just came out that way."

Wordless, she sat across from him, her delicate fingers opening and closing spasmodically as they lay on her discarded poker hand.

Best get this over with, Clayton thought. "What's your second question?" he inquired in a voice gone annoyingly hoarse.

Her mouth opened, closed, opened again. The tip of her tongue slipped out to wet her lips, and his groin tightened. He had told the truth; he did want her. He just hadn't realized how much.

"My second question," she began in an unsteady voice, "is…oh, dear. You see, I had my second question thought out before I asked the first."

"That so?" Clayton wondered why his throat felt so dry all of a sudden. He reached for his coffee. No help there. He sweated marbles waiting for her to finish.

"My second question is—well, I had no idea you would respond in such a manner, so my second question was—is—why?"

Clayton caught her gaze and held it while something inside his belly began to uncurl. *A man can't trust himself when a woman's involved,* his father always said. *So don't get tangled up.*

Why *did* he want Irene Hardisson? It made no

sense. She was attractive, yes. But so were many women.

She was unavailable—maybe that was the pull? But there'd been others, even married women, who'd been "unavailable."

The truth.

What was the truth? Now that he was faced with the frank question she'd framed, he found he had to probe inside himself to answer honestly.

"Truth is," he heard himself murmur, "I hardly know the why of it. I just know deep down that I do. Want you."

"In what sense do you mean 'want,' Mr. Black?" Her voice trembled ever so slightly, but she looked him straight in the eye. She had guts, he'd give her that.

"In the physical sense." A rush of heat in his chest confirmed it. He wanted to fold her into his arms and never let go, unbutton her dress, lift her petticoats and touch her. And more. An arrow of flame shot down his backbone. Lord help him, molten fire shimmered in his veins.

"Why?" she repeated. Only her voice, low and throaty, betrayed other than an academic interest. And her hands. Her fingers shook as she cradled her coffee cup. "Tell me. No one, no man, that is, has ever said such a thing to me. I find it—" she hesitated "—unnerving."

Clayton swallowed. "You're a lovely woman," he said quietly. "More than just pretty. You're like a fine, proud horse, in a way. Like Rebel, my horse. He's got heart and spirit and—" his throat closed for an instant "—a great beauty, inside and out."

Irene stared at him, and then she smiled. Her lashes came down, dark lace fanning her cheeks, and her face flushed rose.

"Thank you," she whispered.

"Irene, I think I'd better turn in for the night before we get into real trouble."

"Yes," she agreed. "You should. I should. But I don't want to, not yet. I want to play another hand. I have thought of another question."

"You might not want to hear the answer," Clayton breathed.

"And," she reminded, "I might not win. *You* might."

Without a word, he gathered up the cards and shuffled them as best he could with his stiff arm. To his surprise, his bad shoulder felt better than it had for days.

"Cut the cards."

She did so. He found himself looking into her eyes as he dealt the hands. He could drown in those large, cool green orbs, drown in her scent, her voice. He sensed he was drifting toward a whirlpool of emotions he'd never felt before—desire tinged with something akin to awe.

Whoa now! She's only a woman, he reminded himself. *Yes, but a woman unlike any other.*

From the depths of his soul, Clayton considered the razor's edge on which he now teetered. It had to do with living and dying, but damned if he could figure out how. He was uneasy. Off balance.

And it was all mixed up with Irene and his smoldering need for her, a complex, overpowering male yearning for this woman who no way in hell could fit into his life.

More on edge than he liked, Clayton stood up and strode to the window Irene had propped open to catch the night breeze. The warm, summer-scented air pressed in on him. In the silence, faint laughter drifted up from the hotel lobby. A wagonload of lumber rumbled along the street below.

Leaning one hand on the sill, he maneuvered his injured arm out of the sling and gingerly flexed his elbow. Pain not too bad. He could ride if he had to.

Frogs croaked in the still night air and Clayton leaned forward, drawn by the sound. The primitive, pulsing rhythm reminded him of nights in Texas when he lay under a black canopy of stars, feeling at one with the earth and its creatures, wondering what a man's life was all about. Now he was beginning to know the answer to that mystery, and it scared the daylights out of him.

In one swift motion he discarded the sling, folded it into a floppy square and stuffed it into his back pocket. Better to face whatever was coming as a whole man. With two good arms, he could mount a horse, he reminded himself.

Or hold a woman.

Chapter Fifteen

Irene watched Clayton draw in a deep lungful of the soft night air and gaze up at the ceiling. He seemed restless, driven by an inner tension that radiated from his lean form. She felt it half a room away, and her senses responded with a thrumming inside her own body, strong as a heartbeat, silent as midnight.

He folded the sling as if ridding himself of an encumbrance, and then he turned toward her. She gasped at the change in his demeanor. He didn't look cool and assured, as he had during dinner and their poker game. The expression in his eyes was oddly hungry. Vulnerable.

She swallowed over the catch in her throat. Assured, she could deal with. Forceful, determined, even headstrong she could deal with. But not vulnerable.

She wondered at herself, questioned why she felt

so drawn to him. Was it because of the barely read-
able emotion she detected in his eyes? An expression that said *Need me* and *Don't touch* at the same
time?

She wasn't seeking pleasure, she reminded herself. Only justice for her client. And truth. She
longed to know the truth about this mysterious man
who now folded his long frame into the chair opposite her.

And the truth about herself. It had taken her a
long time to become the person she wanted to be—
Irene Hardisson, Attorney-at-Law. Now she suspected there was more, much more, to discover
about herself—not as a lawyer, but as a person. A
woman.

Why had she been unaware of this inner dimen-
sion until now? Never hungered for anything beyond a challenging legal tangle or a verbal battle
within the protected walls of a courtroom?

All at once she longed for the familiar home she
had left in Philadelphia, for Nora, the housekeeper
who had raised her after her mother died. Irene had
felt safe rocked in the bosomy woman's soft arms.
Nora knew her through and through.

Now, watching Clayton's eyes darken as he
fanned his cards, Irene suppressed a bolt of pure
joy.

She liked him. She didn't know why, did not
even care. Oh, the outside aspect of the man, the

easy, graceful way his body moved, the quiet, thoughtful manner in which he spoke—such were sufficient for interest, or even admiration. He was, after all, attractive in a rugged, rawboned way with his long black hair and calm gray eyes.

But what had this to do with *liking* a man? She had never liked a man before, other than her father, whom she had adored. It was not adoration she felt for Clayton Black, but something else. Something she could not name.

"Penny for your thoughts?" he inquired with a wry grin.

Irene jerked her attention back to the game. "You will have to win the hand before I divulge one single thing." She hoped her tone sufficiently light to mask the sudden pounding of her heart.

"Spoken like a true gambler." His voice, too, sounded studiedly calm. But his eyes betrayed him. The glance he flicked at her made her breath catch.

More was at stake here than a poker hand. Beneath the usual banter between card players, the polite discourse between a gentleman and a lady, simmered a deeper, more urgent message. An intimate message.

Win truth. Win me.

"Need cards?"

She shook her head. She didn't want him to notice how her fingers trembled.

He discarded two, drew new ones and frowned. "I bet one."

Irene blinked. If she raised him, would he fold? Would he guess she was bluffing on a very thin hand?

He would, she decided. He was the teacher, she the pupil. She had won the previous hand on the sheer dumb luck of the draw, and they both knew it.

"Call." Afraid to breathe, she waited to see his cards. If he won, she would forfeit more than an honestly answered question. An instinctive, visceral jolt to her insides told her she would be offering a private part of herself, offering it to a man who might then know her more intimately than any human being had before. In a sense, he would own a little bit of her. She was terrified.

And exhilarated. A part of her *wanted* to belong to him!

"Three nines," he said, his voice low.

Irene's heart turned over. In silence she laid her cards facedown on the table. "I am afraid I must fold. Your question, Mr. Black?"

He pushed his chair back on two legs and surveyed her with a boyish grin. "Well now, that's more like it. It's not often I get to cross-examine an attorney, so I'll just think on it a minute."

Irene squirmed. Her entire body went hot, then cold. *Ask!* she pleaded silently. *Get it over with.*

Clayton caught her gaze and held it for a long minute. "You know," he said finally, "it's not what happens to people in life that's important."

"It isn't?" she replied in a whisper.

"It isn't. What's important is what they *do* about it."

"I see."

Clayton smiled. "No, you don't," he said softly. "I'm going to put my soul on a plate here and offer it to you in the only way I know how." He raked one hand through his hair and cleared his throat.

"A man can do something in an instant that will bring heartache for the rest of his life," he said, holding her gaze. "I sure hope this isn't going to turn out that way. Irene, would you do me the honor of sleeping in my bed tonight?"

She struggled to hide her shock and the instant flush of happiness that tore through her.

"No," she said simply. Clasping her hands in her lap, she raised her eyes to meet his. "But I will invite you into mine."

She studied his face, saw disappointment turn to amazement.

"Did you say what I think you said?"

"Yes. But do not ask me why. I am learning that it is much easier to react honestly than it is to think about the whys and wherefores."

"A very un-lawyerlike sentiment," he said with a lopsided grin.

"Yes, isn't it?" Her voice no longer shook. She had invited a man into her bed, but because it was *this* man, Clayton Black, she was not frightened. Shy, perhaps. But not frightened.

At least not of him. After all, they had already spent most of one night together in her bedroom, and even though things were quite circumspect, it had established a bond of trust between them. He had not forced himself on her, and she knew that he would not do so. Whatever was to happen now would be up to her.

Clayton took one last dazed look at the cards in his hand, cupped his palm above the painted glass lamp chimney, and with a quick breath blew out the flame. Shaking his head, he slipped the gathered deck into his trouser pocket. She'd held three jacks—the winning hand!

Why would she lose the game on purpose? He could think of no logical reason, unless...

With an inward chuckle he tipped his head back and gazed at the shadowed ceiling. *Why, the little devil!* She wanted the same thing he wanted, but she wanted *him* to do the asking! Amazed and immensely pleased, he pondered the unlikely situation.

No matter how old he got, he would never un-

derstand a woman—especially not this one. Irene
Hardisson had a soft, enticingly rounded body
clothed in flounces and fripperies like a woman,
but she also had a mind like a steel bear trap. The
combination was enough to confound any man.

He did understand one thing—*she* wanted this
as much as he did. The realization brought a hot,
shaky feeling to his insides. He was losing his head
over this woman.

Well, so be it. But he'd make damn sure he
didn't lose his heart as well.

In the darkness, he heard the click of the armoire
door catch and the rustle of Irene's skirt as she
undressed. His hands moved to his belt buckle.
Suddenly he wanted to simply lie down next to her,
inhale her scent.

"Irene."

A swish of petticoats and then silence. He got
rid of his boots, then unhooked his belt. While he
undid the trouser buttons, he listened to her unsteady breathing.

Moonlight dappled the floor, turning it into
etched marble. The *critter-critter* of night insects
was broken only by the faint sound of a horse plodding along the street below. A pounding, like
someone hammering on a roof, began, lapsed, began again. Clayton figured it must be his heart.

"Irene," he said again. He liked the feel of her
name on his lips.

"I'm here," a low voice responded. The armoire door swung shut and there she was, silhouetted against the wall. "I'm dressing for bed."

"Don't," he managed. He could just see her, a glimmer of pale skin, a waterfall of dark hair about her shoulders.

"Don't put anything on."

"Nothing? Not even—"

Clayton thought his heart skipped maybe three beats. "Nothing."

He discarded his trousers and underwear and started to unbutton his shirt. She said nothing, just stood motionless as he came toward her. When he was so close he could feel her warmth, he reached out one hand and touched her face. "You've never done this before, have you?"

"No," she breathed.

"You want to change your mind?"

"No. Do you?"

Clayton smiled into the dark. "I sure as hell don't."

She turned her face into his hand, pressed her lips to his palm. A shock wave rippled up his arm.

"Do that again," he said. With his other hand, he slipped another shirt button free.

She obliged, and he slid his now-tingling palm to the back of her neck and moved forward. His shirt hung open. He pulled her head to his chest, tangled his fingers in hair soft as thistledown. Her mouth opened and a little sigh escaped, wafting warm, moist air against his breastbone. He caressed her temple with his thumb, then positioned his lips near her ear.

"Touch me."

Her hand came up and she spread her soft, cool fingers against his chest.

"Your heart is beating terribly fast," she whispered.

"Damn right." He found he could barely speak.

"Shall I take off your shirt?" She didn't wait for his answer, but ran both hands up to his shoulders and pushed the garment down.

"I have never touched a man before. Like this, I mean."

Clayton caught her hand. "Do you like it?"

"I am not sure. I think so."

He laughed softly. "Try some more," he invited.

"No," she said. "I want...I want you to touch me."

He sucked in his breath. For the past hour he'd been aching to reach for her and do just that.

Very slowly he laid one finger at the base of her throat. Under his skin he felt her pulse throb. He drew his hand downward, toward her nipple.

Suddenly she raised herself on tiptoe, thrusting her breasts upward until they nudged his chest. He curved his fingers over them. Smooth as warm silk, they swelled under his touch.

Her gasp of pleasure sent a red-hot poker into his belly. *Now,* he thought. *I could take her now.*

He shook his head to clear it. No, he couldn't just take her. It was her first time, and not only that, it was as if it was *his* first time, as well. *Lord, how he wanted her!*

He hesitated, made himself think about her, about what this might cost her. And what it might cost him. At the realization he began to shake. No doubt about it, this was unlike any encounter he'd ever had with a woman before. He felt...protective. Responsible.

Scared.

Irene trailed her fingers over his shoulders, down his back, around his waist while Clayton tried to keep his breathing steady and control the trembling in his limbs.

"Double B ranch," he said in a quiet voice. "East of Allenville."

Irene's head lifted. "Why are you telling me this?"

He bent his head and caught her mouth under his. Her lips moved under his, her tongue quick and shy. When he could think clearly again he spoke into her hair.

"If there's a child, you'll know where to find me."

He kissed her again, going deeper, feeling her strain the length of her body against his. "Irene," he said in a hoarse whisper. *Lord, she made him crazy!*

"Irene. *Irene.*"

He lifted her into his arms and moved to the bed.

"Yes" was all she said, but she said it over and over, her lips never leaving his as she returned his kisses.

Chapter Sixteen

Long after the moon had set, Clayton lay awake with Irene wrapped in his arms. He thought about the unexpected passion that simmered beneath the surface of this unusual woman, recalled her moans of pleasure, her joyous, totally female response to his touch, and—most surprising of all—her cry of ecstasy at the moment of fulfillment, followed by uninhibited weeping in the wake of her release. In his entire life, he had never been so moved.

She was like fire and storm underneath. Even nestled sound asleep beside him, her chestnut hair spread over the pillow and her breath blowing gently near his ear, Clayton acknowledged he was awed by her.

He still trembled inside from their lovemaking. His satisfaction had been complete—more than complete. It had rocked him to the depths of his soul. But rather than sink into the drowsy stupor that beckoned, he lay beside her wishing the night would never end. *How,* he questioned himself over and over, knowing her, and himself, as he did at this moment, *how could he ever let her go?*

It bore thinking on, yet he knew there was no solution. The murder trial would end; she would stay in Crazy Creek and build a new life, and he would ride south and take up his old one. Even granting that he would be acquitted of Brance Fortier's murder, as he now expected since Irene had presented hard proof of his innocence and made such a jackass out of the prosecuting attorney, even then, he had nothing to offer a lady of Irene's caliber.

Rangering is no life for a woman. And neither was a hardscrabble ranch in a remote East Texas valley. What could such a place offer to an educated woman with Eastern breeding and social graces?

Flat-out nothing. *Nada. Rien,* his mother would have said. Besides, he had never been the marrying type. He dared not even consider such a thing.

He eased onto his back, covered his eyes with one arm. His discovery of Irene was sweet and bitter at the same time. He wanted her. He could have her for only a moment.

But it was a wondrous moment, one he would remember for the rest of his life.

The hammering sound began again, and Clayton

opened his eyes. The gray dawn light outside the window turned to peach and then rose, and the pounding continued. It wasn't his heart—the noise came from outside. What in thunder—

With care he slipped his arm out from under the soft, warm woman at his side and padded to the window. At the end of the street, in the square formed by two intersecting roads, some kind of structure was being erected. Two men nailed planks together as fast as they could wield their hammers.

He puzzled over what they were constructing. It looked like some kind of crude platform....

His mind went numb.

Irene appeared beside him, a white muslin night robe hastily pulled over her bare shoulders. "What is it?" she whispered. "What are they doing at this hour of the morning?"

Clayton drank in a gulp of the sweet morning air. "Building a gallows," he said quietly.

She made a small sound and he pulled her into his arms.

"It can't be," she said, the words muffled against his neck. "The jury is not yet deliberating."

"Maybe. Maybe not. My guess is the hanging committee wants to be ready, just in case."

"Clayton," she said, her voice unsteady. "Close the window."

He did so, shutting out the ominous sound. Then he gathered her up in his arms and carried her back to bed.

''Gentlemen.'' Judge Phipps addressed the jury in a weary tone. Over the past four hours, the courtroom had gradually filled to standing room only as everyone—townspeople, ranchers, hired men, merchants, even Lysander Pettigrew—all crowded into the hot, muggy room awaiting word on the fate of Clayton Black.

One man held up a copy of the *Crazy Creek Reader.* ''Accused Murderer Awaits Verdict,'' the newspaper headline pronounced in sixty-point type. ''Prosecutor Concedes Defending Attorney Hardisson's Evidence Valid.''

''Thank the Lord,'' Irene murmured aloud when she glimpsed the front page. Clayton's life would be spared.

After last night, that was all she cared about, that he be alive and safe. She refolded her hands in her lap for the twentieth time in the past hour and risked a sideways glance at her client. When he caught her gaze, she found she could not look away.

Irene's breath caught. She had come to him last night, amazing herself by her audacity and her female hunger for him. Most incredible of all, she did not feel undone or ruined, as she always thought a deflowered virgin would. Instead, she felt whole and wonderfully alive. She had come to herself as a woman, opened up her soul and looked inside to see a being she hardly knew before now.

Her body was weary, but her spirit floated, exulted, *reveled* in the gift of physical love between a man and a woman. How much of life she might have missed!

And would continue to miss from now until the day she died. Still, it had been worth it, this uncovering of her secret self. Even when Clayton left for Texas, as he surely would before nightfall now that the jury announced they had reached a verdict, even then she would be glad for what they had known together, however brief.

The judge cracked his gavel for silence. "Gentlemen of the jury, have you reached a verdict?"

The spokesman, a spindly shopkeeper by the name of Solomon Reidel, rose and self-consciously cleared his throat.

Irene let her gaze roam over the hushed spectators. Mr. and Mrs. Brandt sat together, as they always did, holding hands with their gray heads bent toward each other. A knot of ranch hands rocked their chairs back on all four legs and turned their attention to the jury box.

And the mysterious woman with the embroidery hoop continued to thrust her needle in, out, in, out as she had since the opening day of the trial. Irene craned her neck to see the needlework pattern. Some kind of monogram, stitched in black and crimson.

A chill went up Irene's spine as she watched the woman jab out her stitches.

"We have, Your Honor." Solomon Reidel paused and ran a freckled hand over his beard. "Indeed we have."

Irene tore her gaze away from the embroidery lady in time to see the jury members straighten in their chairs. In a matter of moments, Clayton would be free.

Judge Phipps leaned forward, cradling the gavel head in his palm. "And how do you find the defendant, Mr. Black?"

A sudden movement caught Irene's attention. The woman pushed her needle into her design and slowly let the hoop descend to the lap of her black dress. She did not raise her head, but sat as if made of stone, her eyes on the floor.

A hand closed at Irene's throat. Something was not quite right.

Motionless, the embroidery lady waited.

Irene pressed Clayton's arm and with her eyes gestured at the woman in the front row. He studied the still form for a moment, then gave an almost imperceptible shrug.

"Looks kinda familiar," he intoned. "But I don't—"

"Will the spokesman read the verdict?" Judge Phipps interrupted.

"I will, Your Honor. Just give me a minute to collect myself." Solomon coughed into his fist, then deliberately unfolded a small square of white paper.

"We find the defendant, Clayton Black..."

Irene sucked in her breath and held it. *Not guilty,* she prayed. *Oh, God, let him be found not guilty.*

"Yes? Come on, Sol—spit it out."

Beside her, Clayton's breathing grew raspy.

Solomon cleared his throat again. "Clayton Black is—"

Irene gripped her hands together and closed her eyes.

"—guilty."

A moment of stunned silence, and then came a chorus of raucous cheers. "Well done, Sol!" someone shouted. "That shows what Crazy Creek folks stand for!"

People stood, jostled into the aisles as Irene struggled to remain calm. She shot a look at her client.

His lean jaw was set. Through lips pressed tight, he uttered a single terse sentence. "Better make me a will."

"A will!" She practically screamed the word. "Are you crazy? Something has gone terribly wrong. You're not guilty! We must appeal. We'll—''

"Irene." He gripped her hand, pulled her down next to him. "A will. And do it quick. This whole town's thirsty for blood."

She stared at him, unable to utter a single word. A dark haze seemed to settle over everything before her—judge, bailiff, the jubilant spectators.

Gradually her vision cleared and she focused on the embroidery lady. An odd smile twisted the woman's scarlet mouth, but her pale cheeks shone with tears.

Irene's heart jolted. Something was amiss. Something she couldn't begin to name, something she knew had to do with Clayton. But what? *What?*

She felt his hand close around her upper arm. "You all right?" he asked in a low tone.

"No." Dazed, she leaned into him, let him steady her trembling body. *Clayton, guilty? This can't be happening!* It was a terrifying nightmare. Any moment she would wake up and find him beside her. Safe.

"I'm guessing I'll spend tonight in jail," he said. "And in the morning…" His voice stopped. "Get those papers ready for me, will you?"

"But—"

"Just do it, Irene. There isn't much time."

"Clayton?" Her throat closed. "Clayton, I—" The words choked off.

"Don't talk. Only makes it harder. Go on back to the hotel and eat something. I've got some thinking to do."

"I can't! You must know I couldn't swallow a thing."

"Do it anyway," he ordered. "Pour a shot of whiskey in your coffee and send the rest of the bottle over to the jail." He squeezed her arm. "It'll be all right."

The bailiff clumped toward them, handcuffs dangling from his belt. "Sorry, Black. Back to your cell."

Clayton straightened. "Don't bother with the manacles, Jase. I'm not dangerous."

"Like hell," the bailiff muttered under his breath. But he left the cuffs off, and for that Clayton was grateful. He needed his arm free to steady Irene.

She turned her head into his shoulder. He lifted off her hat—the one with the cherries on it—and smoothed her hair. "Go on, now. I'll see you later."

She clung to his arm. "How can—?"

"I said I will, Irene, and I will. He grasped her shoulders and set her apart from him, wondering why he felt so calm. Maybe he was numb. Maybe he just didn't believe what had happened. Or maybe—as in the beginning—he just didn't care anymore. He'd sort it out later with the help of some whiskey. Right now, leaving her was tearing up his gut.

"It wasn't enough to prove your innocence," she said in a strangled tone. "To clear you, I should have discovered the real murderer!"

"You're a lawyer, not a detective," he replied gently.

"Maybe out here in this godforsaken place one should be both!"

Clayton chuckled. "That'd be a combination, all right. Pinkerton would give an arm and a leg to have you and me."

"C'mon, Black. Get on over to the jail." The bailiff's meaty fist shoved him from behind. "March!"

"Go to hell," Clayton said in an even tone.

"I'm warnin' you, Black. As an officer of this here court, I can—"

Clayton cut him off with a gesture. Tipping Irene's face up, he brushed her ear with his lips. "Don't forget the whiskey," he whispered.

She nodded.

"About the will," he reminded. "My full name is Clayton Joshua Black. Leave the space for the beneficiary's name blank."

She nodded again. He squeezed her shoulder and lifted his hand away from her warmth.

It was one of the hardest things he'd ever done.

* * *

After downing three fingers of the quart of Child's Premium whiskey Irene sent over from the hotel, Clayton acknowledged what he hadn't wanted to see before. Come sunup, he was going to die.

That being the case…he ran his finger around the lip of the bottle…*he'd better make his move now, while he was still sober enough to think straight.*

First off, he'd have to steal a—

Hold on a minute! You're not just gonna up and leave! There was the matter of his will, and…well, his will was a good enough reason. Truth was, the thought of riding out of here without seeing Irene—even to avoid the gallows—was not possible.

He'd never lay eyes on her again. Never laugh at that silly hat she wore, never touch her or hear her low, musical voice saying his name, or…

The hell he wouldn't! It'd be a risk, but he'd rather die than miss the chance. She'd be at the hotel. Said she couldn't bear to return home until it was all over.

He waited until nightfall. From his cell he watched Sheriff Calder's head droop lower and lower until it finally plopped onto the papers stacked up on his desk. *Now.*

Without a sound, he swung his legs off the cot, bunched up the mattress under the thin, moth-eaten blanket and stepped to the window. One hard shove on the hastily installed bars and the iron grill scraped across the crumbling adobe sill and came free. Making no sound, he levered his body through the opening and slipped out into the night. Staying in the shadows, he made his way down the alley to the Maybud Hotel.

Hellfire, the place was lit up like Christmas! Laughter and the tinkle of crystal washed over him, and he breathed out in relief. The noise would cover the sound of his boots on the roof.

He grasped the eave and swung his torso up onto the upstairs porch. Four long steps and he stood at the window of Irene's hotel room.

"Who's there?" a tentative voice called.

He didn't answer. With slow, deliberate motions, he hooked one knee over the sill and stepped quietly into her room.

She met him before he'd taken two steps. In silence he folded her into his arms. "I couldn't leave without seeing you," he murmured against her hair. The scent of her skin under the silky nightgown made him ache.

"Clayton—" Tears glistened on her cheeks.

He bent, stopping her words with his mouth. He kissed her hungrily, then framed her face in his hands and rested his lips against her forehead. It was sweet, so sweet, to be with her.

"I have to go," he said at last.

She tipped her face up. "I know."

"I love you, Irene."

He hadn't meant to say it, thought it better left unspoken under the circumstances. He'd never told a woman that before, and it scared him. It scared him a lot.

But he had to tell her. He'd never see her again, and she had to know how he felt before he rode out. He'd sign his will and write in her name as beneficiary. If they caught him, killed him, he wanted her to have whatever was left—the ranch, the herd, the land—everything he'd put his hand to.

Gathering a strength he didn't know he had, he set her away from him. "It's time."

"It's hours yet before dawn," she whispered.

"Got to latch onto a horse somewhere. It's best done in the dark."

"If they catch you, they'll shoot you for a horse thief!"

Clayton chuckled. "There's worse things. Hanging's one of them."

He heard her quick intake of breath. "If I make it to Texas, I'll write."

"Yes. Oh yes, please do."

"You can reach me at the Double B ranch, Cherokee County. If I'm lucky."

"Oh Clayton..." Her voice caught on a sob.

"I love you," he said again. "Dammit, don't forget me."

"You know I won't." Her voice shook. "Sign your will. I'll see that it gets—" She pressed a pencil into his hand.

He kissed her, hard, and moved to the open window. In the faint moonlight he scribbled her name and his signature on the single sheet of paper.

He kissed her again and held her, peering out the window over her head. In the street below stood a horse.

"Well, I'll be a—" He gave a low whistle, and the animal pricked up its ears. "Rebel," he breathed. "Be there in a minute, boy—don't go away!"

"Your horse?" Frowning, Irene stared down into the street. "Clayton, something is not right. Why would your horse just turn up like this?"

"It's strange, all right. But it saves me having to steal one, so I'll take the risk."

Without another word, she began to unbutton her nightgown. "I'm coming with you." She moved to the armoire and the door clicked open.

"Like hell you are."

"Clayton, it's a setup. A trap!"

"So it's a setup. Once I mount that gelding, no one on God's green earth's gonna catch me. Reb can outrun the wind."

Irene said nothing.

Clayton took a deep, agonizing breath. "So long, honey." He slipped through the sash frame and stood up on the second-floor porch.

Irene flew to the window and leaned out. "You fool," she whispered.

"Probably," he acknowledged as he stepped to the roof edge. "Better than hanging, though. Remember me, Irene. I'll sure never forget you!"

"Idiot!" Irene hissed. "Wait for—"

But he dropped off the roof onto the street below, and in the next instant the sound of horses' hooves broke the stillness.

Two horses. Clayton's and another one, following at a distance.

Irene clenched her fists. God in heaven, it *was* a trap! She turned away and tried to think.

Chapter Seventeen

Clayton heard the horse behind him, acknowledged what he had suspected when he first glimpsed Rebel in the street outside the Maybud Hotel. He'd stepped into a trap.

It was clear someone had been watching him, anticipating his moves. Whoever it was trailed him now at the same slow, steady pace he set for himself until he was clear of town. No use making a ruckus and rousing another posse—they'd miss him soon enough.

He scanned the sky above him. He had about three hours, he figured. By daylight they'd be coming after him.

Only one good thing, he thought as he tightened his fingers on the reins. He was headed north, not south as they would expect.

And the second set of hoofprints would throw them off.

For a while.

Who in tarnation was the rider behind him? His neck prickled, but he resisted the urge to turn around. *Just keep moving, nice and easy, until you can make a break for it.* Up ahead, maybe. Near that clump of cottonwoods.

He held his breath as he drew near the feathery trees, slowed for a split second, and then dug the mare hard in the ribs. *Now, Reb! Let's go home!*

He kneed the horse and struck out to the southeast. The gelding stretched his long legs, and Clayton risked a backward glance at his pursuer. What he saw knocked the breath out of him.

A woman! Riding astride, her black skirt billowing, she stuck to him like a cocklebur for a mile or so, then began to fall back. Who the hell—

A bullet zinged past his left thigh.

"I will kill the horse!" she shouted.

Another shot whistled by, waist-high. She wasn't kidding! She was aiming for the gelding, not for him—otherwise, she'd shoot higher. What kind of person would shoot a horse to stop the rider?

Someone desperate. Another shot echoed, and Reb squealed in pain and danced sideways. Clayton looked back to see blood glistening on the animal's rump.

Maddened, the horse began to run. Instead of moving with the gelding's motion as he usually did, he tightened his legs and buttocks. The horse would feel it right through the saddle and would—he hoped—begin to slow. To keep the bit loose, he pulled alternatively on each rein, then concentrated on turning him into an ever-decreasing circle. When he'd gotten his attention, he began to talk. "Easy, boy. Easy now."

The horse began to slow. Carefully he drew rein and waited.

"Good," a feminine voice purred. "I have followed you long enough." She stepped her mount forward. Clayton's gaze moved from the white, set face to the barrel of the revolver she held in her gloved hand.

"Dismount, if you please," she ordered.

Clayton obliged. The instant his boot met the ground, he turned his back on her and the gun she held. "Excuse me, ma'am, but I need to tend my horse."

He inspected the animal's wound. The bullet had creased the hair and ploughed through some of the flesh. He tugged the saddle blanket free and pressed it tight against the bleeding. While he worked, he kept one eye on the woman.

She was tall, too slender for his taste. Under the black dress her bones looked to be hard and angular. He'd swear he didn't know her, but she kept watching him and smiling as if she expected him to say something. Worse, she kept the revolver trained on him every second.

He finished with the horse, wiped his hands on his pants. "If I didn't know better, ma'am, I'd say you got me out here in the middle of nowhere on purpose."

She laughed softly. "Now, Clayton Black, what am I to do with you, talkin' that way?"

"You want a suggestion? Put that gun away and tell me what this is all about."

Her thin eyebrows arched. "About? Why, darlin', don't you know?"

Clayton's gut tightened. "What I know is that you purposely shot my horse, and I don't take kindly to that. Also I'd guess you're Southern," he observed in a terse voice. "But that's about it, other than you're a good rider and maybe a fair shot. I don't aim to test your skill in either area, so why don't you just explain what's going on here?"

He started toward her, but she waggled the pistol and he halted. Damn fool woman would blow a hole in him if she wasn't careful.

"You don't recall me, do you?" she pursued, her voice turning silky.

"On the contrary," Clayton replied. "You're the lady in the courtroom, with the embroidery."

"Oh, I'm much more than that. Don't tell me you don't remember?"

"Remember what?" He racked his brain. Had he ever seen her before the trial? Did he know her from somewhere in his past? She was attractive enough, but not the kind of woman he'd seek out for himself, or the kind he'd remember if he had.

"Five years ago, at your mother's plantation. Your grandfather gave a midsummer ball. You were there."

He had a vague memory of a dance one warm summer night, ladies in soft white dresses, plenty of whiskey, fiddle music, perfume. He hadn't danced with anyone. Hadn't even talked to anyone except his grandfather, Etienne Varlon. They'd talked about horses, he recalled.

"I was there, too," she said softly. "I had a beautiful new silk taffeta gown. I was beautiful. Everyone said so."

Clayton frowned. "I'm sure you were, ma'am."

"All the men wanted to dance with me," she said dreamily. "All except you." She narrowed her eyes. "Why was that, Clay? Why did you always avoid me?"

"Hell, ma'am, I don't even remember you. If you say I avoided you, I must have had a reason."

"Oh, there was a reason," she retorted. "A very big reason, clinging to me all evening. My brand-new husband. It didn't stop the other gentlemen, but you were different."

"I don't court married women."

She rounded her carmine lips into a pout. "But I begged and begged you, don't you remember? I knew he wouldn't mind if *you* walked me out. Brance was afraid of you."

Clayton's mind froze. "Brance? Brance Fortier?"

"Sure and certain, darlin'. The man you're accused of killing." Her dark eyes glittered oddly. "It's Estelle, honey. You remember now, don't you?"

It all came back to him, the teasing hands, the invitations to dance with her...and more. Brance Fortier's wife! Instantly his senses sharpened.

"What are you doing out here, Estelle? Why aren't you back in New Orleans where you belong?"

She took a step toward him. "I've been following you. Ever since you cornered my husband in your momma's yard that day, ever since you set out after Brance, I've been following you."

He'd known it. Felt it inside him. All those months on the trail he'd sensed someone behind him, not pressing, just...there. Sometimes he figured it was his conscience.

"Why?" His voice was hard.

Her eyes widened. "Why? I'd think that would be apparent to a man as smart as you, darlin'. I want revenge. Sweet, slow revenge."

The way she lingered over the words sent a needle of ice up his spine. "Estelle, I'm sorry about what happened to Brance. Sorry I had to track him, sorry he's dead. But I didn't kill him. I swear to God, I—"

"Oh, I know you didn't, Clay. And you needn't be sorry he's dead. He's not."

She took another step toward him. "He's not dead at all. The man they found on the north trail road that night wasn't Brance. It was someone else."

Clayton's blood ran cold. "Not dead? Estelle—"

"Oh, don't say anything more about it. There's something else I want now. Something I've wanted every single night since that summer when you refused me. You'll be sorry you did that—say no to me. No one refuses Estelle Fortier."

Clayton's entire body tensed. She made sense in the way a crazy person made sense—logical to a point, but not grounded in reality. She was dangerous, a loose cannon.

"What do you want, Mrs. Fortier?"

She spoke with quiet venom. "I want to make you pay for what you did."

His first reaction was to laugh. *For what he did?* But not for shooting her husband, as he had thought. *For ignoring her one summer at a dance?*

"I know where Brance is," she continued, her voice tight. "I know he'll come lookin' for you. I wanted to be sure I found you first. You owe me, Clay honey. Watching you suffer will be payment in full.''

He had to get that revolver away from her. He stretched out his hand, palm up.

''Give me the gun.''

''Oh, no, darlin'. Not on your life.''

''Then pull the trigger and get it over with.''

A peal of laughter broke from her lips. ''But it's not *you* I'm going to shoot! Why, how can you even think it?''

Cold horror knotted his stomach. ''Who, then?''

''Just you wait and see,'' she murmured. ''It shouldn't be long, now. I thought of it today, while I watched you.''

Clayton stared at her, fear gnawing his brain. Desperately he tried to think. If she wanted him dead, all she had to do was squeeze her forefinger. That she had not done so told him she wanted something else, wanted to make him suffer some other way. Like a mad dog, she would go for his naked underbelly. Either that, or she intended to use him to get at someone else.

When he heard the faint sound of hoofbeats in the distance, he knew. At the realization, every nerve in his body recoiled.

God in heaven, he wished they'd hung him back in Crazy Creek.

* * *

Irene reined in the horse and paused to get her bearings. She knew she was on the right track—she'd watched Clayton ride north out of Crazy Creek rather than south, as the sheriff would expect. Once she figured out her client's strategy, she knew she could catch up.

Eventually. First she'd had to dress hurriedly and acquire a mount. She suppressed a shudder. At the moment, she didn't want to think about that.

It wasn't difficult to find where Clayton had turned into the creek that encircled the town; the muddy banks near the livery stable showed two sets of hoofprints. She, too, turned into the creek and stepped her horse south, backtracking to skirt the edge of town as Clayton had done to avoid leaving a trail for the sheriff. She even took off her borrowed Stetson hat and scooped water over the telltale prints on the creek bank—including those made by her own mount.

By the time she was on her way again, the sodden hat dripped water down her neck and her hastily done up French twist had come loose. She must look a sight!

She splashed on down the creek, exiting only when she was certain the double set of tracks in the dirt were the right ones. In a way she was grateful for the horseman who followed Clayton; two sets of tracks provided a more noticeable trail in the faint moonlight. Inexperienced as she was at such things, were it not for the second horse, she might lose their trail.

Neither rider ahead of her was being particularly careful, she observed. Bushes were mashed along the way, protruding twigs broken off. The two were easy to follow.

Irene frowned. With extra caution she stepped her horse forward. It was a handsome animal, a small gray that turned out to be as gentle as it looked. Still, her heart hammered beneath the hurriedly donned white percale waist she wore with her riding skirt.

Just what do you plan to do when you catch up to them? She had not one inkling. Improvise, she guessed. Surely, two heads—hers and Clayton's— would be better than one!

And, she reminded herself, she had her pistol. She'd dug the derringer from the bottom of her travel valise and loaded it with fingers that shook. She carried it now in her skirt pocket, within easy reach of her right hand.

Could you bring yourself to shoot someone? A lump of hard coal settled in her throat.

She could for Clayton, she assured herself. For Clayton, she could at least try.

When she heard the gunshot, her body froze in the saddle. Up ahead, beyond those trees.

Two more shots, then silence. Irene patted the

gray's warm neck. "Thank you for not bolting!" she murmured.

She guided the mare toward the sounds. As she advanced she heard voices—a man's low tones mingling with...*a woman's*? Irene stepped her mount forward until she could see.

Clayton stood in a small clearing, one hand on his horse's rump. A tall figure in a full-skirted black dress faced away from Irene, pointing a revolver at Clayton's chest.

Irene opened her mouth, then thought better of it. Quietly she slid the derringer out of her pocket and cocked the hammer. The click sounded like a cannon shot in the silence, but to Irene's surprise, no one moved. Clayton saw her and shook his head imperceptibly.

"She would not dare shoot," the woman drawled. "If she misses, she'll hit you."

Irene blinked. *She?* How did the woman know it was a *she?*

"Join us, won't you, Miss Hardisson?" the soft, sultry voice continued. "We've been waiting."

"Waiting?" Irene gasped. "For me? How could you possibly know—"

"It wasn't so difficult. All I had to do was watch Clay, see the way he looked at you in court this past week. I followed him when he left the jail tonight, and I wasn't at all surprised when he high-tailed it straight to you."

"Hush up, Estelle," Clayton growled. "How'd you get here, Irene?"

Irene gulped. She kept the pistol trained on the woman's back, but she knew she didn't dare fire. She'd never fired a gun in her life, and her hand wobbled.

"I...well, I found a horse and—"

His eyes widened. "You *found* a horse? Where?"

"Oh, all right, I...um...borrowed it. Took it." Perspiration started under the high collar of her waist. "I guess I...stole it," she finished in a small voice.

His laughter startled her.

"It isn't the least bit funny," she protested. "I have committed a...a crime!"

The woman called Estelle slowly pivoted to face her and Irene's heart stopped. The embroidery lady!

"Why, my goodness gracious, a lawyer *and* a horse thief! Clay, you do have the most unusual taste in women."

He ignored the remark. "Irene, you are the prettiest damn horse thief I've ever known." He spoke slowly, and at the same time began moving away from his horse. His steady gaze held hers, and then, still grinning, he signaled his intentions.

He wanted her to keep talking while he circled

behind the woman, evidently planning to wrest the revolver out of her hand. Irene took a deep breath.

"I never expected to…I mean I did not intend— you see, the horse was just standing there near the hitching rail in front of the hotel. That is, he was tied up at the hitching…"

Out of the corner of her eye she gauged Clayton's stealthy progress. Just five more steps and he'd be close enough. "So I wrote a note and stuck it—"

The embroidery lady laughed. "You left a note? My, oh my, but that's rich! May be that you are a lawyer an' all, but y'all don't seem very bright to me. A note!"

Suddenly her eyes narrowed. "I don't think I believe you," she snapped. "Sure and certain—"

Clayton tackled her from behind and they went down in a tangle of boots and petticoats. Shaking, Irene tried to keep the derringer trained on the woman on the ground, but the two thrashed and rolled so violently she hesitated to press her finger on the trigger for fear of hitting Clayton.

And then a gun did go off—but it wasn't hers. Horrified, she watched Clayton lurch to his feet. He held the woman's revolver in his hand, but on his thigh a dark stain spread. Irene's stomach turned over. He was hurt.

"Clayton!"

"Watch her," he ordered. He pressed his fingers to his leg and winced. "Flesh wound. I hope."

The woman scrambled to her feet and headed for her horse. "Stop!" Irene shouted. "I'll shoot!"

"No, you won't," she said. Grabbing the pommel, she hauled herself ungracefully into the saddle and scrabbled for the reins. "You're too much of a lady."

Clayton started toward her, but after a single step, he stumbled and fell to his knees. "Let her go," he rasped. "We can track her later."

"You'll have to catch me, Clay!" Estelle screamed at him. "I dare you to try it with a bullet in you!"

She wheeled the horse away. "Better say your prayers, darlin'. You're still gonna hang for murder!"

With a vicious jab she spurred her mount and galloped off into the night.

Clayton got to his feet and stood before Irene, swaying slightly. "Help me mount," he directed. "We've got work to do."

Chapter Eighteen

Irene kept her mare's nose close to the hindquarters of Clayton's dark gelding. The trail was too narrow to ride abreast, and anyway she doubted she could keep up the pace the ranger set. Riding astride rather than sidesaddle, as she was used to, her back muscles screamed in protest and her thighs were beginning to chafe. Western horses were so much more rambunctious than their Eastern counterparts!

When she borrowed the saddled horse she found tied to the Maybud Hotel hitching rail, she had not realized that. She only hoped whoever owned the animal she now bumped along on would not miss it before morning.

Ahead of her, Clayton grunted and bent low over his mare's head. She could barely see him in the dark.

"What are you doing?" she called.

"Studyin' the ground for trail signs."

"In this blackness? I can scarcely see my hand in front of my face."

He straightened in the saddle. "Keep your hand on the reins, Irene. A horse gets uneasy when a rider fidgets."

"I'm not fidgeting, I'm trying to stay seated. And awake," she added in a lower tone.

"We'll rest come sunup," he said over his shoulder.

Sunup! Her heart sank. "How long will that be?"

"One, maybe two hours."

She said nothing. Two more hours of this and she would barely be able to move, much less dismount.

"If we stop now, the sheriff and that posse of shopkeepers will catch us. They'll shoot first, talk later—if we're still alive. You savvy?"

Irene shuddered. "Yes." She hoped her voice did not sound as frightened as she felt. They had to keep going. Under the protection of darkness they could travel undetected; at daybreak, a mounted figure, even a puff of dust, would be seen for miles.

"How is your wound?"

Another grunt from the blackness. "Hurts like...hurts. Bleeding's stopped, though."

"There is danger of infection," she reminded.

She heard him chuckle. "Better than a bullet in the back." He turned abruptly to the left. "Follow close. Trail's gonna climb."

Climb! It felt like Jacob's ladder made of slippery rocks going straight up the mountain. She urged her mare forward and caught her breath as the horse tilted under her.

"Lean forward when you're goin' up," Clayton called. "Easier on the horse."

She didn't want to lean, she wanted to stop. She was sweaty and frightened and confused. But she knew that Clayton could not turn back toward Crazy Creek. The sheriff would hang him before he could explain about the trap the embroidery lady had led him into.

The more Irene thought about the woman, the more she puzzled. There was something unbalanced about her, something calculating and sinister under the Southern manners. The hair on her neck rose at the memory of her voice, silky on the surface but so full of venom.

Why was Clayton so bent on catching up with her? She'd shot him once already. Surely this was another cleverly laid trap—one in which Estelle would lead Clayton to where Brance Fortier was hiding and then the two of them planned to finish him off.

But, Irene thought with a wave of satisfaction, they wouldn't expect *two* riders. Estelle would as-

sume Clayton had sent her back to town and was
coming after her alone. Therefore, she reasoned, it
was vital that she keep up with him. Uphill, downhill, it didn't matter. She could not let him walk
into another trap alone.

His voice carried over the sighing night wind.
"You okay?"

"Y-yes. Fine," she managed. She would not admit how tired and thirsty and just plain scared she
was.

"Trail's gettin' clearer. She must be gettin'
tired."

How, Irene wondered, could he see anything at
all in this blackness, let alone know whether his
quarry was tired? Clayton displayed uncanny
skills. If she—they—got out of this nightmare
alive, she would ask him about this—and about
other things she had noticed. His hair, for instance.
She had never seen a man with jet-black hair almost to his shoulders. It gave him an exotic, almost
savage look.

"She turned off here," Clayton said. "Headed
downhill."

Irene braced herself for a descent. "Will it be
very steep?" She wasn't sure she could stay seated
on a steep incline.

For a long minute he made no answer. Then he
reined in and waited until she caught up to him.

"We're not goin' down after her. I want to be above them. We'll keep on till daylight."

Relief warred with fear in her brain. On? Did that mean up or down? She had no sense of where they were—whether high on a mountainside or deep in a canyon. She disliked not knowing exactly where she was. Her city breeding, she supposed. In Philadelphia, every street had a name; all buildings had numbers. Out here there were no landmarks. It was like being in limbo.

The sky lightened to gray and then peach. Clayton increased his pace. He knew Irene was exhausted; he was plenty tuckered himself, what with his leg hurting like it did. But he didn't dare stop until the sun was up and he could see. Damn if he wasn't squeezed between a rock and a hard place as Pa used to say. A killer ahead of him, a crazy sheriff's posse behind. At least when it grew light, he could watch for riders on the valley floor and see into the canyon he sensed was directly below them.

The delay gave him time to think. He was right where he wanted to be. He'd corner that bastard Fortier and avenge Pa and Jannie's murder if it was the last thing he did in this life. Oddly, he wasn't worried about the outcome. He'd get Fortier or die trying, it was as simple as that.

One thing did bother him. Irene. Having her along complicated things, made him wary of taking risks he wouldn't think twice about if he was alone. He didn't want Irene in danger. His biggest fear was that she'd get hurt—or even killed, like Jannie. He hadn't been able to save his sister. He had failed her and himself by not being sufficiently in control and clearheaded to anticipate Fortier's moves. He couldn't live with himself if he failed Irene, too.

He thought again about sending her back to town, then dismissed the notion. He couldn't ask her to face a sheriff who wouldn't understand how she "borrowed" a horse to ride after him. And that posse of his—hell, they'd shoot her before she got close enough to tell she was a female.

He guided Rebel into a copse of scrubby, wind-sculpted cedars and looped the reins over a limb. Slipping off the horse Indian-style, he tried to land soft, but when his boots met the ground, he lost his balance and fell. Couldn't seem to move his leg.

Dried blood crusted his pant leg. He'd have to stop and take a look.

Irene dismounted. She looked stiff and uncomfortable and kept one hand at her backside as if it hurt. Probably did. He remembered she wasn't used to Western saddles. He untied the canteen at his belt and offered it to her.

Moving gingerly, she made her way to his side.

"Should we not save the water to wash your wound?"

"Got alcohol for that." He unscrewed the metal top. "Drink slow."

She tipped up the canvas-covered container and water dribbled down her dirt-smudged chin. While she drank, Clayton unsheathed his knife and sliced open his trouser leg.

He groaned at the sight. There were two holes in his flesh—one where blood welled up and another, larger hole with a ragged edge where the bullet had exited. Flesh wound, but dirty. He'd have to clean it out.

He motioned over his shoulder. "In my saddlebag. Bottle of whiskey and a leather pouch." His field first aid kit. He never went anywhere without it. Funny that Rebel would show up with the saddlebag untouched. Course he never carried any money; all his bounties and Ranger salary were paid into the bank at Allenville.

Irene unstrapped the bag and rummaged in its depths. After a moment she returned with a bottle of spirits and the pouch.

It was light enough now to see. Time to get on with it. He tested the knife blade with his thumb.

Irene watched him with widening eyes. "Wh-what are you going to do?"

"Clean my wound."

"Shouldn't you sterilize your knife?"

He looked at her. Practical to the core. She didn't waste time arguing about the inevitable.

"Yep. But I can't risk a fire—the smoke would be visible for miles." He doused the blade in whiskey and set his jaw.

"You'll need bandages." She flipped up her riding skirt, bent and snagged something white—her underdrawers, he guessed—with her teeth. With efficient motions, she bit a thread and ripped the lace edging off the hem.

Clayton sucked in a deep breath and dug his knife point under the oozing scab on his thigh. Fire laced across his skin, danced against his thighbone.

When his vision cleared, he saw oily yellow liquid seep through. He'd have to scrape it out.

He knocked back a jolt of the whiskey, clenched his teeth and began to work. Slowly, methodically, he dragged the blade through the wound again and again. Tears stung into his eye, but he made no sound until it was over.

"Pouch," he gasped. Before he could hesitate, he dumped more whiskey into the bloody depression. The alcohol ate into his flesh.

"Hellfire and brimstone," he hissed.

Irene opened the leather pouch and drew out a handful of crumbly gray-green material. "What is this?"

"Tree moss," he groaned. He slapped a handful onto his thigh and pressed it down. In silence she handed him the strips of lace from her underdrawers and watched closely as he bound the moss in place.

"That looks like an Indian remedy," she said.

"It is."

She turned abruptly and stood with her back toward him, arms locked over her stomach. "Are you finished?" she asked in a small voice.

He rose unsteadily, took another pull at the whiskey and sheathed his knife. "Finished. Now let's see if anyone's picked up our trail."

Irene blanched as Clayton stumbled past her, moved to the canyon edge and peered over. Dragging his injured leg gave him an off balance, lurching gait. If he slipped on the gravelly ridge…

She averted her eyes. She couldn't think about it.

But you have to think about it, she reminded herself. No one in his right mind would be up here in the first place.

She was bone-tired. Her temples pounded with each beat of her pulse, and her backside felt like it had been drubbed up and down on a washboard. Whatever had possessed her to follow Clayton out of Crazy Creek? She'd even stolen a horse to help him!

It was perfectly obvious she was not in her right mind. In fact, she admitted, her emotions—her whole life—had been upside down ever since the day Clayton Black stepped into her office.

She watched him kneel at the canyon lip and study the view over the edge. Was it the destiny of women to follow some man hell-bent on risking his life on a quest to settle a personal score?

Lex vincit, her father had taught her. The law will conquer. *Maybe back in Philadelphia, Papa, but not out here in the West.* Frontier justice, she was learning, could go awry. Still it was the only sensible way to settle disputes. She believed law prevented the strong from always having their way. That was what distinguished civilized order from anarchy.

What would it take to tame such a wild, lawless land?

What would it take to tame a *man* with the same uncivilized nature?

Tame him! What nonsense was she thinking? She had to use all her feminine intuition and brain power just to understand him.

She studied his back as he knelt, motionless, at the canyon edge. There was only one law-abiding way out of their present dilemma, she realized.

She moved to his side and spoke softly. "You have to go back, Clayton. Give yourself up. And then…" She hesitated. "Then you will be free."

Clayton remained motionless. "Can't do that," he said over his shoulder. "Posse'd shoot me on sight. Besides, Estelle isn't sitting in the witness box telling the judge what she knows. She's down there with Fortier.''

Irene knelt beside him, careful not to get too close to the cliff edge. "You can see them?"

"In that little draw, beyond those two big boulders. They're holed up in a cave, but there are signs. Her horse, for one thing. It's picketed a ways off."

Irene studied the land below them. Try as she might, she saw no sign of life—no campfire, not even the horse. Clayton must have eyes like an eagle.

"Got to find a way to separate them," he muttered.

"Separate them? What on earth are you contemplating? They are waiting for you down there, and you're walking right into their clutches. Would it not be smarter to—"

"Nope. I've got a score to settle with Brance Fortier. Only problem is how to get you out of here in one piece."

Irene bristled. "Don't think for one minute that I'm leaving you alone up here!"

"That is exactly what I'm thinking. You're in over your head."

"And you're not, I suppose? With your leg crippled and a murderer—and his accomplice—lying in wait? Why, I never heard of anything so fool—"

He rose in one swift motion and pulled her to her feet. "You think too much. You do exactly as I say, or neither one of us will come out of this alive."

"I will do no such thing."

His eyes burned into hers. "Yes," he said quietly. "You will. In a courtroom, you know best. Out here—" he gestured at the surrounding rocks and juniper scrub "—I do."

"I cannot argue that, Clayton, but this is a matter of justice. One cannot simply hunt one's enemies down and kill them. It's barbaric."

"Fortier killed my father and my kid sister. It's more than justice—it's a matter of honor."

Helpless in the face of his logic, she searched for something to say. "An eye for an eye, is that it?"

"Something like that. All I know is I've got to call him out."

"No!"

He turned toward her, grasped her shoulders with both hands. "Honey, you've got two choices for the next twenty-four hours. Stay quiet and out of sight or tear up some more of your underclothes and ride back to Crazy Creek under a white flag. Which'll it be?"

"I won't go back. I can't leave you."

"Then stay out of the way and let me do what I've come to do." He kissed her, quick and hard. "And don't think for one minute," he said against her hair, "that this is the way I wanted it. I can't stand the thought of something happening to you."

She caught his deerskin vest in both her hands and clung to him, her head pressed against his chest. The smell of him—horse and sweat and man—made her dizzy with longing. What had happened to her to make her feel so wanton?

You've fallen in love, that's what. With a man likely to live no longer than another few hours. She clenched her fists across her stomach. What earthly good were feminine emotions if they led to such pitfalls! She loved a man who valued his honor over his life.

She thought about leaving him on the mountain, riding back to town to convince Judge Phipps that Clayton was innocent. But she knew she'd never make it in time. Sheriff Calder would already be on their trail, and he would never listen to her plea to turn back. Some men were like that, she acknowledged. Stubborn. Unwilling to bend.

Clayton was one of them. Men like him were the ones that got themselves killed. A bullet in the back or a hangman's noose, it made no difference. Dead was dead.

Her stomach gave an uneasy flutter. She cared about him and her caring made no difference. He was set on revenge. The flat, hard look in his eyes, the set of his jaw told the whole story. He would never give up until the matter was settled, one way or the other.

She felt helpless and angry and more at sea than she'd ever felt in her life. Did Estelle feel this way about Brance Fortier? Perhaps not.

Irene's mind reeled. Estelle was an unknown quantity in the equation. Unpredictable.

Merciful heaven, what should she do? She was completely out of her element, away from lawbooks and legal precedents. She had nothing to fight with.

But at least she had a choice. She could watch Clayton die, or she could think of some way to help him.

She had about twelve hours, she calculated. Clayton would stay hidden until dusk. *Either way, you'll lose him,* a voice reminded. *Even if he gets through this alive, he'll head for Texas, not for Crazy Creek and me.*

Still, no matter what he did, she wanted him to live. She wanted him to have the choice.

All at once she thought of Papa. She knew now why her father never remarried. Loving someone spelled heartache.

They huddled in the shade of twisted cypress and scrub pine, saying little. Clayton went over the plan he'd worked out in his mind. Bad luck not to have a gun. He'd have to leave that little pistol of Irene's for her protection.

But he had a knife, and a length of good rope in his saddlebag. That'd have to do. Fortier would expect a direct assault. Instead, Clayton would surprise him.

They shared the water until the canteen ran dry. Irene tried to nap, but her throat was so parched she couldn't keep her thoughts on anything but her thirst. Clayton dozed in the mottled shade, his back against a tree trunk. When she'd fidgeted for an hour, he reached for her. Without opening his eyes, he pressed her head down onto his lap and smoothed her hair.

"Don't think about it," he murmured. He laid his hand over her eyes, blocking the sun, until she grew drowsy. She dreamed of water, a cold, clear stream so close she could smell it. She woke with her throat on fire, her tongue swollen and furry.

"They're comin'," he remarked. "Posse's picked up our trail."

She looked across the brown valley and saw dust puffing into the air. Tiny figures on horseback— six of them—picked their way forward, moving slowly but inexorably nearer.

"How long?" she croaked. Her mouth felt as if it were stuffed with dry thistles.

"Sunup tomorrow, if they bed down for the night. Otherwise…"

"Tonight," she supplied.

He nodded. "We're caught in a pincer. Have to make my move before midnight. Fortier's seen them, too. He's waitin' to see which trail they follow—Estelle's or ours."

"And then?"

"Then Fortier will wait to see what I do next—go for him or the posse."

The back of her neck prickled. "What do we do?"

"Wait. Don't move around and kick up any dust."

Wait! She thought she'd jump right out of her skin she was so frightened. *How can he be so matter-of-fact when his life hangs in the balance?*

"Another three hours," he murmured. "Think you can handle it?"

"Yes," she lied. Another three hours and she'd die of thirst. At least a bullet would be quick.

"Not gonna die," he observed as if reading her thoughts. "Comes to it, we can drink horse piss. It'll keep us alive."

Irene shuddered. Horse piss! Bullets! Deranged Southern ladies. What was her life coming to?

"It's not so bad," Clayton said with a chuckle. "Kinda salty, though."

"How can you joke at a time like this?" she flared.

He ruffled her hair. "Nuthin' else to do. Too

shot up to make love to you. Nothin' else worth doin'. A day like today, the sun feeding the life growing out of the earth, feeling you warm and soft in my arms, the wind whisperin'—it's as good a day as any to die.''

Irene jerked. "You said we're not going to die!"

"You're not. I might."

"Clayton," she pleaded. "Tell me your plan. Let me help."

He focused on the straggly line of riders on the valley floor. "Can't. Not all of it, anyway. It won't help me if I'm worrying about you gettin' hurt. When that posse decides which trail to follow, I'll tell you what to do."

In spite of herself, Irene raised her head to watch the progress of Sheriff Calder and his men below them. *Please, God, let Sheriff Calder follow Estelle's trail, and not Clayton's.*

The party of riders halted and Irene watched the lead man mop his face with a red bandanna and gulp from his canteen. Her throat ached at the imagined taste of the water.

Under the scorching sun, the line of men moved forward. Clayton stiffened and leaned forward.

The posse bypassed the cutoff and headed up the mountain, straight toward them.

Chapter Nineteen

Estelle Fortier dug the toe of her boot into the ribs of the man sleeping beside her. "Brance, wake up. I hear horses."

He was on his feet in an instant. Pausing at the mouth of the cave, he scanned the route Estelle had used. "You left enough of a trail," he grumbled. "A child could track you here."

Estelle flinched. She didn't know which man she hated more—her husband or the Texas Ranger who was hunting him. Neither man wanted her. She didn't care which one of them died—she knew only that she wanted Clayton to suffer.

Brance turned to her. "It's all working out, just like I thought, Stel. Black's gonna hang for murderin' me. Boy, that's rich, isn't it, honey? I'm alive and Black's gonna hang."

"You're sure of that, are you?"

"Real sure. That posse's turning off. Must be

following Black and that lawyer lady you told me about. Soon as we hear the shots, we'll backtrack outta here and head for the border.''

Estelle looked at him and tried to smile. "Sure, Brance. Just like you said. We'll start a new life.''

Her heart felt as if it were made of lead. She didn't want a new life in a strange town. Not with this man.

But at the moment, she had no choice. She'd done what he wanted—set Clayton up for the murder charge, planted subtle suspicions here and there among the townspeople to make sure he got convicted. Now there was one more thing she wanted to do. Something she'd thought about during the trial. Something even Brance wouldn't be expecting.

She picked up her embroidery hoop and began viciously jabbing her needle in and out of the smooth, white linen.

By dusk, the sound of horses struggling up the steep incline was so close Irene could feel their hoofbeats reverberate on the ground beneath her. She sat up straight and glanced at Clayton.

"They're very close," she ventured.

Clayton dipped his head in a subtle nod. "Not yet. Timing has a lot to do with the outcome.''

"Calder's posse is practically on top of us!''

Clayton looked at her with steady gray eyes,

then turned his gaze across the valley. "You ever think about a rain dance? What it signifies?"

"Clayton, in heaven's name, what has that to do with the situation we're in?"

"Timing, like I said."

Irene stared at his profile so hard her eyes burned. The man had more layers than one of Nora's ribbon cakes. She never knew what to expect, and now he sat here calmly talking about a rain dance while men came to capture him. Or kill him, she added with a shudder. She bit her tongue and tried to remain calm.

A tense quarter hour passed. By now, she could hear the horses panting, hear their hooves scrabble on the loose rock. At last Clayton heaved himself to his feet.

"I want you to keep down and keep quiet. When the posse gets here, point your pistol at Sheriff Calder and talk to him first, quiet-like. Then stand up slow so they'll see it's you."

He laid his hand on her shoulder. "I never loved a woman before, Irene. I'm never going to forget you." He gave her a searing kiss, then set her apart from him.

"Adios."

"Wh-what are you going to do?"

"A rain dance, honey. If I don't get back, tell them about Fortier."

She couldn't speak.

He limped to the canyon edge, knelt down and disappeared over the edge. She listened to his slow, unsteady footfalls until she could hear nothing but the soft moan of the wind.

Suddenly she was terrified. With that leg wound, he could barely stand up, let alone walk steadily. She couldn't just sit here, letting her mind imagine all sorts of terrible things. She had to do *something*.

She waited until the wheezing of a winded horse told her the sheriff had reached their mountaintop lookout. She had to act, and it had to be now.

With a mumbled prayer, she inched toward the cliff. If Clayton could negotiate it with a wounded leg and only one good arm, she could certainly manage. When she reached the crumbling lip, she bundled up her riding skirt in one hand, grasped a protruding tree root with the other, and scooted her derriere over the edge.

It took the better part of an hour for Clayton to reach the cave entrance. He glimpsed the flicker of firelight from deep within and suppressed a chuckle. Fortier still liked his coffee hot. He'd stumbled upon the still-warm ashes of the killer's campsites all the way from Texas to Idaho. Maybe he hadn't realized Clayton was gaining on him.

Maybe he hadn't cared. Could be that explained who shot him off his horse. He'd seen only a shadow, then the flash of the gun.

He flexed his gun hand. All in the past, now. He'd come to settle the score.

"Fortier," he called. "You hear me?"

"I hear ya," came a voice from inside the cavern. "Been expectin' you, Clay."

"You're under arrest, Brance. For killing Jannie and Pa."

"Prove it."

Clayton moved closer. "Don't have to," he said. "I saw you do it."

Fortier laughed. "You're a dead man, Clay. You're gonna hang for murderin' me. That's how Stel said she made it look."

Clayton frowned. "You tellin' me Estelle put a bullet in a man's back?"

"I'm tellin' ya."

No woman he'd ever known would shoot one man to frame another. He'd pegged Estelle right the first time he saw her. She was more than unhinged. Brance's so-called wife was just plain loco.

Clayton spoke into the darkness. "You're gonna pay for everything you did."

He knew Fortier heard him from the sudden quiet inside the cave. "Which way you want it, Fortier—custody and a trial down the road or a showdown here and now?"

Silence. Then the click of a safety catch being released.

"Come out with your hands reachin' for the clouds," Clayton called.

"Not on your life."

He drew in a long breath and released it through clenched teeth. "Then I'm gonna have to kill you."

"I know you, Clay. Give me a fair fight."

"Agreed." Clayton stepped into the shadows and waited.

"I'm comin' out." Fortier appeared at the cave entrance. Even in the semi-darkness, Clayton could tell the man was thinner than he remembered. His movements were still catlike, though. And Fortier's trigger finger had always been twitchy—that's how he'd survived his years with the Cortina gang. He and Pa had chased the remnants of that bunch all over hell and gone, picking up bodies as they went. If they hadn't ended up in his mother's front yard, maybe Jannie…

The old rage slammed into his gut. One more step. One more step and he'd get his chance to settle up with Brance Fortier.

"You out there?" Fortier yelled. "Speak up, so I can find you."

"I'm here." Clayton tightened his grip on the knife as Fortier turned toward him. He held a rifle.

"Can't hardly see ya, Clay. Too dark."

Clayton stepped forward. Head up, shoulders

straight, he fingered the blade in his hand. "On the count of three."

"Clay, your pa didn't give me a chance."

"One."

"I had to shoot him. Had to."

"What about Jannie? You didn't have to kill her. You didn't have to drag her off and—" He took a steadying breath. He needed every ounce of control he could muster.

"Honest, Clay, I—she asked for it, boundin' outta the house that way."

"Two. I'm gonna kill you for that. Get ready."

Fortier stood stock-still.

"Thr—"

"Clayton!" A woman screamed. "Behind you!"

He dropped to the ground and rolled sideways. Pain jolted through his thigh.

The shot ploughed into the dirt at his back. Instinctively he brought the knife up.

"Drop it, Clay darlin'," a silky voice ordered. "Do it, or I'll shoot your lady friend instead. Come on out, Miss Hardisson."

Irene stumbled into view and Clayton groaned. "Thought I told you—"

"Yes, I know," Irene said. "But I couldn't. I just couldn't. I thought you might need some... well...help."

Clayton got to his feet. "Leave her out of this."

He stepped between Irene and Estelle, who leaned against a waist-high lump of granite, pointing a rifle at his back. *His* rifle, he noted. He recognized the hand-carved stock.

Inch by pain-filled inch he moved backward, toward Estelle, talking at every step. When he figured he was close enough, he jackknifed at the waist and barreled into her.

The rifle flew out of her hands and she fell headlong against the boulder. Clayton grabbed the gun and whirled to face Fortier. What he saw made him groan aloud.

Fortier had Irene pinned in front of him, one arm clasping her waist, the other yanking her shoulders against his chest. "Got me a hostage here, Clay. You do like I say and she won't get hurt much."

"You blood-sucking bas—" Oh, God, it was Pa and Jannie all over again. But this time he had to tame his fury. He had think real clear. And he had to win.

Clayton fought to harness his temper. Now more than ever before in his life he needed to be coolheaded. If he made one false move, Irene would die and his life wouldn't be worth a plug of tobacco.

He forced himself to slow down and think. He'd play for time.

"Okay, Fortier. Your call." Very slowly, he raised the rifle and aimed it at the left side of Fortier's chest, just above Irene's shoulder. He wouldn't shoot if he didn't have to. But knowing Fortier, sooner or later he'd have to. Fortier would push his advantage until there would be no other recourse.

Behind him, he heard Estelle approach, felt her arms slide around his middle. "That wasn't nice, darlin'," she purred. "I got mah backside all bruised up falling over that rock."

"Sorry." Clayton spoke without taking his eyes off Fortier and Irene. It was so dark now he couldn't tell where her shoulder left off and Fortier's chest began. Fat chance he had of winging him.

Estelle tightened her arms about his waist. "What do you say we kiss and make up, Clay?"

He sucked in his breath as an idea took form. It was a long shot. Maybe Fortier would want his woman back enough to let Irene go. "In front of your husband?"

"Sure, honey."

Clayton turned to Estelle. "Just say the word."

She slid her arms up around his neck. "Now, darlin'," she whispered. "Now."

Irene gave a strangled cry. "Clayton Black, you lay one hand on that woman and I'll...I'll never speak to you again!"

He damped down an irrational urge to laugh and pretended to ignore her. Instead, he slipped one arm around Estelle and pressed his mouth to hers. But he kept his eyes open, the rifle pointed at Fortier.

Irene's mouth opened into a surprised *O*. Her eyes widened and then darkened to the black-green of a Texas thunderhead. Giving a sudden squeal, she bounced upward, knocking her head soundly against the underside of Fortier's jaw.

Clayton seized his chance. "Dance!" he shouted.

She caught his meaning in an instant and began to jiggle and flail her arms about. When Fortier ducked a flying elbow, she stomped one foot down on top of his and twisted to one side.

It was the moment he'd waited for. He squeezed the trigger.

The bullet nicked Fortier's neck.

"Why, you son of a—" With a vicious wrench, he jerked Irene's arm in back of her. She didn't utter a sound, but the twist of her mouth made Clayton's stomach turn over.

One more shot. He needed just one more shot. And this time he knew he couldn't afford to miss.

"I see it," Sheriff Jim Calder muttered as he peered over the edge of the canyon. "I just don't believe it."

Below him in the gathering dusk he could make

out four figures—two of them women. "What the Sam Hill…"

Clayton Black stood holding a rifle with a lady in black sprawled at his feet. The other man, a stranger—thin and mean looking—was trying to hold on to a lady who'd apparently gone loco.

The sheriff frowned. "Now that don't make too much sense," he muttered. "Why would a man wanted by the law be holdin' a gun on that stranger down there? Unless…

"Git up there, Sandy!" He gave his mount a jab with his spurred boot. "Let's go, boys. That's what we came fer, to catch a killer. Looks like we got 'im."

"Horsemen!" Fortier yelled. He yanked Irene backward toward the cave entrance.

"Sheriff's posse," Clayton said in a quiet voice. "Watch 'em. They're a bunch of trigger-prone amateurs."

The two men stared at each other as the first horse broke through the brush.

"Black?"

"Sheriff Calder," Clayton acknowledged. "Thought you'd never get here."

"Both you men, put up your weapons!"

Neither Fortier nor Clayton moved a muscle. On the ground, Estelle began to sob. "That man is Brance Fortier." Her words came out in jerky hiccups, and Clayton heard the unmistakable tone of hysteria in her voice.

"That so? What makes you so sure, ma'am? Way I understood it, Fortier's s'posed to be dead."

"He's my husband. He's wanted for—"

Fortier jerked. "Shut up, Estelle."

She made a choking sound. "He—he killed Clay's fath—"

With a growl, Fortier thrust Irene away from him, gripped his rifle in both hands and fired. Estelle's body arched and then sprawled in the dirt at Clayton's feet.

Dropping to one knee, Clayton laid his rifle on the ground and bent over her. Sheriff Calder knelt beside him.

"...killed his father and sister," she gasped. "Oh, Clay, hold my hand."

He grasped her fingers and squeezed.

"That man," she whispered. "The one they found on the town road? I was the one who shot him. I wanted to hurt you, Clay. Wanted you to hang instead of Brance."

"Jehoshaphat, ma'am, you know what you're sayin'?"

She smiled weakly up at the sheriff. "Oh, yes, I know." She turned her gaze on Irene, who now crouched at her other side. "It's the truth."

Fortier lunged forward. "So help me, I'll kill her," he swore. "And you, too, Clay."

Out of the corner of his eye Clayton glimpsed the flash of a silver belt buckle and reached for the knife at his waist.

A bullet zinged past his ear. Without conscious thought, he loosed his blade.

Fortier stumbled forward and collapsed.

For a long minute, no one said a word. Finally Irene spoke in a calm, tired voice. "You had to do it, Clayton. He would have killed you."

"Lady's right, Black. No blamin' you. Looks like I've been chasin' the wrong man." The sheriff lumbered to his feet. "Posse's bringing yer horses down. Ned, Alastair, tie them bodies on a horse and let's move out."

They rode out of the hills single file, picking their way slowly until the moon rose. Clayton brought up the rear so he could keep an eye on Irene. His thigh wound throbbed, but it wasn't hot to the touch. He thanked his father and his Cherokee grandmother for their teachings. His knowledge of the old Indian ways had kept him alive.

He wondered if there was a Cherokee remedy for love. Something to ease the pain of parting. He knew he had to leave her. He couldn't stomach the thought of being the only half-breed in a cake-frosting town like Crazy Creek. A town built on land stolen from the red man.

A sick feeling flooded him. And she'd never survive on a ranch in dry, dusty East Texas.

He closed his eyes in anguish. Their souls meshed. Their bodies had joined in passion. But their lives would never fit together.

He groaned under his breath. That was the teaching, then. Loving was one thing. Making such a miracle last wasn't so easy.

He felt his separateness, his status as an outsider. The pain now was more keen than at any time in his life.

But it was best this way, he acknowledged. The demands of his kind of life would eventually destroy her, as it had his mother. She and Pa had loved each other, but in the end, his father's harsh, lonely way of life had sucked her dry. She'd ended her days on her father's Louisiana plantation.

Irene, too, needed to spend her life among the civilized.

But oh, God, he'd miss her. He'd miss her all the rest of his days.

The sun was just rising as they clattered onto the main street of Crazy Creek. The sheriff shook Clayton's hand and headed for his office; the posse drifted toward the Silver Swan saloon. Clayton and Irene rode in silence to the prim white house on Park Street.

He helped her dismount. Her body trembled with exhaustion. She leaned into him for a long minute, then tipped her head up. "Clayton, I have made a decision. I cannot remain here in Crazy Creek. Not after this. Not after…us."

For an instant his heart leaped. She'd risk it? Come with him?

"I am going to Portland."

"Portland," he echoed. His voice sounded strange to his ears, as if the words came from someone else.

"To practice law. I must—" Her voice broke. "The sheriff tells me there is a stage leaving at ten o'clock tomorrow morning. I cannot bear to stay here after…without…"

He said nothing, just held her. Lord knows he'd never forget the feel of her in his arms. She pressed her cheek against his chest.

"I love you, Irene." He spoke the words softly, near her ear.

"I know."

He folded his arms around her and kissed her until the blood roared in his head. "Don't forget me."

"You know I won't," she whispered against his mouth. "Ever."

He dragged himself onto his horse and moved

on down the street. His chest felt like a herd of steers had trampled it.

When he reached the edge of town, he looked back. Through a shimmer of tears, he watched her arm lift in farewell.

Chapter Twenty

Promptly at nine o'clock the next morning, Irene waited for the stage in front of the Maybud Hotel. She'd spent the past few hours packing her travel valise and trying not to think. She would wire Nora from Portland about her change of plans.

Without a single word of reprimand, Sheriff Calder retrieved the horse she'd borrowed and carried her luggage to the stage stop. Her heart ached. An aching need had opened inside her—one she had been unaware of until the day she met Clayton Black. The need for a man's love.

She tried not to think about the empty feeling inside. Tried to erase the memory of his arms holding her, his mouth on hers.

For an hour she was unsuccessful, and then she decided it was no use even trying. She would never forget him. Would she had never met him!

Oh, no, she did not wish that. Clayton had

changed her. Brought her to the full flower of womanhood. But she could not think of that right now. She hurt too much to think about spending the rest of her days longing for him.

The stage rattled in right on time. Irene rose, adjusted her cherry-topped straw hat and forced her feet to move forward. When she climbed aboard, she could let the pent-up tears flow.

The driver hefted her valise onto the top rack. "Portland, ma'am?"

She nodded, her throat tight. She settled herself in the empty coach and reached in her reticule for a handkerchief. Dry-eyed and aching, she knotted it around her fingers.

Happiness, she acknowledged with a choked sob, required such a great amount of courage. She must be strong.

The stage jerked and rolled forward.

Clayton rode south for an hour after his morning coffee. Too tired and heartsick to ride farther without sleep, he'd camped in the hills south of town. He hadn't slept. All night he hungered for Irene, and by morning he couldn't stand it any longer. He needed to put some distance between them.

He reached a rise and reined in his horse. Slowly he scanned the valley behind him.

A black stagecoach moved west across the flat plain. The Portland stage. He caught a flash of red from the passenger window and his eyes stung. The woman he loved was hurtling out of his life.

"Rangerin's no life for a woman...."

With a weary groan, he turned away to the south and urged Reb into a canter. He trotted for half a mile and suddenly pulled up short.

Why, you damn fool! You're gonna throw her away because you're afraid of life without the reputation you earned in Texas? Afraid you'll never be anything but a rootless half-breed who inherited a ranch from his daddy?

A picture rose in his mind—Irene leaning toward him, a whiskey bottle in her hand, the cherries on her hat bobbing with the motion of the stagecoach. She'd saved his life. More than that, she'd given him back his soul.

Hell, Irene's worth more than a hundred ranches!

He pulled the horse around and hunched low in the saddle.

"Hang on, ma'am," the driver yelled. "Trouble's comin'."

Irene heard the whip crack and the stage lurched ahead. She clapped one hand on her hat and gripped the seat with the other.

"Bandit, most likely." The driver's raspy voice floated through the side window. "Better hide yer jewelry!"

The vehicle slowed and at last creaked to a stop. Numb, Irene sat without moving.

It doesn't matter. The money folded in her reticule, her rings, even Mama's pearl brooch—none of it mattered. She was dead inside.

Hoofbeats. Then the driver's voice. "Don't shoot, mister!"

The passenger door jerked open. Before she could react, strong arms dragged her out of her seat.

"Clayton! What are you doing here?"

"That hat, honey. I couldn't stop thinkin' about that hat."

Her hat? Dumbfounded, she stared at him.

"Irene, listen. I've got a proposition for you."

She opened her mouth, closed it, opened it again. A more roundabout proposal she had never heard!

Dizzy with joy, she could only nod. "I'm listening," she managed.

"Marry me. We'll settle somewhere, anywhere—halfway between—"

"Yes," she sang, her voice choked. "Yes! *Yes!*"

"—between Texas and Oregon. I'll come north, you come— Yes? Did you say Yes?"

She smiled up at him through a wash of tears. "Can you be a Texas Ranger in Idaho?"

"Nope. I'll go private. Ride for Pinkerton, maybe."

Her eyes shone. "You'd give up your ranch?"

He pulled her close. "For a price."

"Name it," she murmured against his lips.

"You." He raised her onto her tiptoes and closed his mouth over hers.

"And that hat with the cherries on it."

A voice carried from the top of the stagecoach. "Hellfire, folks. You goin' or stayin'?"

After a long minute, they answered in unison.

"Yes."

Epilogue

"Clayton, I have something to tell you."

He looked up from the rolltop desk Irene had given him for a wedding present. Her father's, she'd told him. "Yeah? I've got something to tell you, too."

She gazed out the window, dreamily turning the gold band on her finger. Outside, the clear September sky arched over them like a blue canopy.

"You first," she said, suddenly shy.

"Okay." He faced her. "You're going to have a child."

Her eyes widened. "How on earth did you know that?"

"Indian savvy. Your turn, Mrs. Black."

"Sheriff Calder wrote. He's retiring and they want you to be the new sheriff of Crazy Creek."

Clayton sat so still Irene thought he hadn't heard her.

"Now, that's funny," he said. "Real funny."

Her spirits sank.

He pulled her down onto his lap and smoothed her hair. "Got something else to tell you," he said softly.

"What is it?" She could scarcely concentrate her disappointment was so keen.

After a minute he said, "Nora's got the house ready."

"House? What house?"

"The one in Crazy Creek. The one with the rose wallpaper in the dining room."

Very slowly, she turned to him. "You've known all along, haven't you? About Sheriff Calder."

"Nope. Just a guess. I always liked that house. Knew you didn't want to give it up."

"Oh, Clayton! Oh, I'm so happy!" She hugged his neck. "Oh, darling, we'll wallpaper the nursery in blue!"

"Pink," he countered.

She sat up straight. "Pink! What makes you think it will be a girl?"

He caught her about the waist and pulled her down into his arms once more. "I'm half Cherokee, remember?"

"Yes," she said quietly. "I remember. You're the man who taught me that life is not always predictable. A mix."

"A mix," he mused aloud. "Like a white steeple town and a poker-playin' half-breed sheriff."

"We must settle on a name."

"Yeah," Clayton murmured. His eyes looked shiny.

"Clayton," Irene whispered against his cheek. "I have an idea, a way to decide."

There was a long, long silence. At last, Clayton pressed his lips near her ear and spoke.

"Five-card draw, deuces wild."

* * * * *

Author Note

Some years ago, my husband and I explored an historic old house outside of Canyonville, Oregon. The smallest of the upstairs bedrooms, obviously a child's room, had been wallpapered in a tiny pink flower print. The pattern didn't quite match in places, and the edges were unevenly trimmed, but both of us were simultaneously struck by the same thought: A man and a woman had loved each other, had conceived a child, and had decorated a room to welcome the product of that love.

Some things do not change.

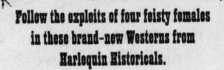

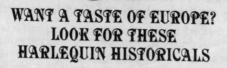

WANT A TASTE OF EUROPE?
LOOK FOR THESE
HARLEQUIN HISTORICALS

ON SALE NOVEMBER 2000
THE STOLEN BRIDE
by **Susan Spencer Paul**
Part of the popular *Bride* series
(England, 15th century)

and

SILK AND STEEL
by **Theresa Michaels**
Sequel to *Fire and Sword*
(Scotland, 14th century)

ON SALE DECEMBER 2000
THE ELUSIVE BRIDE
by **Deborah Hale**
(England, 13th century)

and

MAID OF MIDNIGHT
by **Ana Seymour**
Third in the *Lyonsbridge* series
(Normandy, 12th century)

HARLEQUIN®
Makes any time special ™

Visit us at www.eHarlequin.com   HHMED15

You're not going to believe this offer!

In October and November 2000, buy any two Harlequin or Silhouette books and save $10.00 off future purchases, or buy any three and save $20.00 off future purchases!

Just fill out this form and attach 2 proofs of purchase (cash register receipts) from October and November 2000 books and Harlequin will send you a coupon booklet worth a total savings of $10.00 off future purchases of Harlequin and Silhouette books in 2001. Send us 3 proofs of purchase and we will send you a coupon booklet worth a total savings of $20.00 off future purchases.

Saving money has never been this easy.

I accept your offer! Please send me a coupon booklet:

Name: _____

Address: _____ City: _____

State/Prov.: _____ Zip/Postal Code: _____

Optional Survey!

In a typical month, how many Harlequin or Silhouette books would you buy <u>new</u> at retail stores?

- [ ] Less than 1
- [ ] 1
- [ ] 2
- [ ] 3 to 4
- [ ] 5+

Which of the following statements best describes how you <u>buy</u> Harlequin or Silhouette books? Choose one answer only that <u>best</u> describes you.

- [ ] I am a regular buyer and reader
- [ ] I am a regular reader but buy only occasionally
- [ ] I only buy and read for specific times of the year, e.g. vacations
- [ ] I subscribe through Reader Service but also buy at retail stores
- [ ] I mainly borrow and buy only occasionally
- [ ] I am an occasional buyer and reader

Which of the following statements best describes how you <u>choose</u> the Harlequin and Silhouette series books you buy <u>new</u> at retail stores? By "series," we mean books within a particular line, such as *Harlequin PRESENTS* or *Silhouette SPECIAL EDITION*. Choose one answer only that <u>best</u> describes you.

- [ ] I only buy books from my favorite series
- [ ] I generally buy books from my favorite series but also buy books from other series on occasion
- [ ] I buy some books from my favorite series but also buy from many other series regularly
- [ ] I buy all types of books depending on my mood and what I find interesting and have no favorite series

Please send this form, along with your cash register receipts as proofs of purchase, to:
In the U.S.: Harlequin Books, P.O. Box 9057, Buffalo, NY 14269
In Canada: Harlequin Books, P.O. Box 622, Fort Erie, Ontario L2A 5X3
(Allow 4-6 weeks for delivery) Offer expires December 31, 2000.   PHQ4002

If you enjoyed what you just read,
then we've got an offer you can't resist!

Take 2 bestselling love stories FREE!

Plus get a FREE surprise gift!

LYNNA BANNING

has combined a lifelong love of history and literature into a satisfying new career as a writer. Born in Oregon, she has lived in Northern California most of her life, graduating from Scripps College and embarking on her career as an editor and technical writer, and later as a high school English teacher.

An amateur pianist and harpsichordist, Lynna performs on psaltery and recorders with two Renaissance ensembles and teaches music in her spare time. Currently she is learning to play the harp.

She enjoys hearing from her readers. You may write to her directly at P.O. Box 324, Felton, CA 95018.